WAITING FOR MY BELOVED

By

Sandra Becker

First published in United States in 2017

Copyright © Sandra Becker 2017

D0805225

Table of Contents

1. Let Go and Let God   **1**

2. God Has a Plan for You   **83**

3. God will Show the Path   **148**

1. LET GO AND LET GOD

Chapter 1

"I am so excited!" Ruth exclaimed.

"I know. I am happy for you, dear *Schweschder*," Mary replied.

Ruth looked at her sister Mary and smiled. It was a beautiful morning in Lancaster County. The family had just finished breakfast, and Ruth and Mary were in the kitchen cleaning the dishes. The biggest part of their morning routine was already done. Ruth had woken up at dawn, collected the eggs, milked the cow, and then turned it out to pasture. While Ruth cared for the animals, Mary had gathered vegetables and helped her mother with the breakfast.

"You will follow me soon enough," Ruth

said.

Mary was a year younger than Ruth, and the two of them were very close. A few days before, Ruth had celebrated her fifteenth birthday, and she knew that it meant the advent of *rumspringa*. Most of her friends had looked forward to this as a time to be more social with boys of their age, but Ruth was more excited about the fact that it was also an opportunity to finally become a member of the church.

Rumspringa was a time when teenage boys and girls were allowed a bit more freedom as they began to court and made a formal decision about whether to join the church and agree to live their lives in accordance with the rules of the *Ordnung*, the Amish community order. Ruth had seen some of her friends spend *rumspringa* at home, while others had gone to stay with relatives while they pondered their decision. In most cases, her friends had already made their decision, and they therefore used most of their time during *rumspringa* observing adults, learning from them, and emulating their behavior and values.

Ruth was already learning from her mother the habits and work ethic of a respectable Amish lady. She had a deep faith in God and she knew that this would be her chance to prove her devotion to God.

The dishes were soon done, and Ruth wiped her hands with a cloth.

Mary had a dreamy look in her eyes. "*Mudder* told me that next year it will be my turn for *rumspringa*. I would love to go to the singings and spend more time with the boys."

Ruth smiled. She had felt the same way. She had watched from the aisles as her friends had become church members and started participating in the choir.

She patted her sister on the cheek and said, "Sure. We will have a lot of fun together once you complete your *rumspringa*. *Mudder* will also give you a new dress next year."

"That would be *wunderbaar*. Will you be going to *Ant* Sadie's *haus*?"

"Yes. Father sent her a letter. She said that she would be delighted to see me again. It's been quite a while since we visited her, not since Mr. Schwartz's wedding."

Just then, their youngest sibling, ten-year-old Abram, rushed in. "Look what I found *Schweschder*." He held a frog in his hand.

"Oh! Be careful, you could hurt the tiny animal." She took the frog gently from Abram's hands and released it on the floor. The frog gave a croak and hopped away.

"*Ach*! Mr. Frog is running away." Abram's face fell.

"Don't worry, little *bruder*. Mr. Frog will be around the neighborhood. He knows that we are really nice people. He will come back when he needs our help. Now cheer up. I have a secret to share."

The boy's curiosity was piqued. "A secret?"

"Yes. A secret."

"What is it?"

"I start my *rumspringa* in a few days."

"Oh!" Abram's voice dropped a notch further. "It's not fair. Everyone else gets to see the outside world, but I have to stay at home."

Mary smiled and hugged her brother. "There is so much love here. Why do you want to go anywhere else?"

* * * *

The marketplace was less crowded than usual. It was mid-morning and Ruth had come to the marketplace for two things. One was to trade eggs and milk for some firewood. The other was to meet her friend Sarah. Sarah hadn't arrived yet, so she met the tradesman and traded her eggs and milk for a small pile of firewood. Then she watched the other sellers ply their wares. Neighbors greeted each other and made small talk. It was Sunday, but still a typical day at the market.

Suddenly a young man across the way caught her eye. It was his mustache that got her attention. It was unusual to see anyone in their community with a mustache. Married men wore a beard without a mustache. But this person wore no beard, only a mustache. And the face behind the mustache was handsome.

Her heart stopped. The young man was next to a car, and it looked as if he was asking for directions from one of the vendors.

It's an Englischer.

Her heart spiked as she looked at him. She felt an unusual but irresistible attraction to the stranger.

"Well, well, well." Ruth turned at the sound of the familiar voice and saw Sarah at her side. Sarah glanced at the *Englischer* and then back at Ruth.

"He is handsome, isn't he?" Sarah giggled.

"Yes. He is strikingly attractive," Ruth admitted.

Suddenly, the young man turned toward them, as if he had heard their conversation. His eyes met Ruth's, and for a fleeting moment she felt as if he were reading her thoughts. Then he got into the car and guided it out of the market.

Ruth watched him until he was out of sight. "I wonder what he is doing here?" she said.

Sarah shrugged. "He's probably here to have fun or to make fun of us. Not that I would mind. I am starved for strangers. All we have here are plain-clothed people."

"Hush, you mustn't speak so," Ruth scolded her. "It is God's will that we should dress simply and not be ostentatious. We are the people of the *Ordnung*. We are the ladies of the community. We must do what is right."

Sarah sighed. "I guess you are right." Then her face brightened as she asked, "How are the preparations for your *rumspringa* going?"

"They are going well. I have thought a lot about my future. I have learned so many things recently, especially in the time since I completed school. This will be the first time I will be away from *Mudder* for so long. I am a little nervous about that, but please don't tell her or she will be afraid of sending me away."

Sarah nodded. "I won't tell anyone. I know how it goes. I was scared, too, when I had to leave my family. But I got to live with my *Ant* and I prayed to God to give me strength. I will now pray to God to guide you."

"Thanks, Sarah."

"We have church services at Mrs. Bayer's house today. Do you want to come along with me?" Sarah asked. Church services were held every other Sunday and rotated from home to home throughout the year.

"Sure," Ruth agreed. We will have to stop over at my house first and drop off the wood."

By the time they reached Ruth's home, her family had already left for the services. Ruth put the firewood in the kitchen and she and Sarah headed out. They reached Mrs. Bayer's house a few minutes later.

Most of the community had already gathered for the service. Ruth joined her family, as Sarah made her way over to the choir. The first prayer began in a slow, melancholic tone, praising God's kindness, and everyone joined in.

O Gott, Vater, wir loben dich und deine Güte preisen wir…

Ruth joined in with the others. She silently expressed her gratitude and asked for the Lord's blessings. She thanked God for the wonderful family she had and prayed to God to make her a member of the church very soon.

Suddenly, however, the image of the young stranger flashed through her mind. She shook her head, and redirected her thoughts, a trifle concerned.

This had never happened to her before.

* * * *

Chapter 2

The young stranger thought again of the lady at the market. *Real pretty face. I would like to see her again;* he thought and then shook his head. He knew better.

He went over the events of the past few days that had led him to Lancaster County. Last month, he had been working for a prestigious medical research center in Philadelphia. He wouldn't have imagined in his wildest dreams that he would be in Amish territory only a few weeks later.

It had started with his boss Dr. Jones finding out that he was drinking while on the job. Dr. Jones had confronted him and accused him of being an alcoholic. He had tried to talk his way around it, but it hadn't worked. His boss had only become angrier. A couple of days later, he was given a new assignment. He was to study the genetic effects of intermarriage among the Amish. This would require him to do an onsite evaluation of an Amish community.

He knew the reason why he was selected for this assignment. And it was not for his genetic knowledge. *They wanted me to stay away.*

He thought of the girl and of others like her in the Amish community. *This is an orthodox society. The people won't want to be around someone who binges on alcohol.*

As a doctor, he knew the terrible effects of alcoholism, but its grip on him was beyond scientific reason. He had taken up the bottle after a painful breakup with his girlfriend. The pain of the loss had subsided, but the craving for the bottle hadn't.

So what if I do need a little sip now and then? What right did Dr. Jones have to judge me?

He saw a farm in front of him. It had a quaint cottage with lush green fields spread out around it in every direction. Near the house he saw a tall oak tree next to a shed. It was the landmark he had been told to look out for. *This must be the place,* he thought.

He parked the car a little further from the cottage, walked up to the door, and knocked. An elderly lady opened the door and peered out at him.

"Good morning, ma'am. My name is James Townsend."

* * * *

Emma Byler looked at her children and smiled. *They have grown up so quickly*, she thought.

It was evening, and the sun was nearing the horizon after completing its work of nourishing the farm throughout the day. She watched her eldest daughter, Ruth, playing with Abram and Mary. Their squeals of laughter could be heard from afar. Ruth guided them to the barn and the younger ones sped away, apparently playing a game of hide-and-seek.

"The kids seem to be enjoying themselves, Emma." her husband, Samuel said, coming to stand at her side.

Emma adjusted her prayer *kapp*. "Yes. They are so carefree. It's wonderful to watch them grow up."

Samuel looked out at the fields. "God has

been good to us. We have been blessed with *wunderbaar* children."

"Yes, we have." Emma remembered when each of her children was born. There had been no complications during their births and each time the labor had been relatively pain free. She had seen plenty of other mothers who had to deal with intense labor pain or worse, miscarriages and stillborn infants. She mouthed a silent prayer expressing her gratitude.

A piercing squeal came from the barn. Ruth had just caught Abram. Emma and Samuel laughed.

"Will this happiness last?" Samuel asked, becoming serious.

Emma was surprised. "Why do you say that?"

"It's probably nothing," he said with a

shrug.

"No. Do tell me. You can share your feelings with me," Emma told him.

"Well. It's about Ruth's *rumspringa*."

"What about it?"

"Do you think she will decide to stay in the community?"

Emma smiled. She understood why Samuel was concerned. Some of the younger generation had not become members of the church. They had decided to move out of the community. Some of the community elders had been concerned. There had been some talk about how the children were being influenced by the *Englischers*. But Emma's trust in the Amish way of life was strong. Even stronger was her trust in God. This gave her confidence that Ruth would do the right thing at the right time.

She said, "I trust she will stay in the community."

Samuel breathed heavily. "I am glad you feel that way. Sometimes I worry about her. We have protected our community from outside influence for a long time. However, my greatest fear is that she will one day meet an *Englischer* and leave us."

Emma put her hand on his shoulder. "Samuel, you must not worry so. We have brought up Ruth in a loving and caring way. She has imbibed our values and beliefs. She is no longer a child, dear."

"I know, but I can't shake off a nagging feeling of doubt," Samuel said.

"I have spoken with her about *rumspringa* and she is already committed to joining the church," Emma told him. "I don't think that's the problem. I think I know what you are really worried about, though."

"You do?"

"You are worried about the time when she will get married and leave us. Isn't that it?"

Samuel sighed. "I guess you are right. I can't bear to see her leave us. The five of us together are a family. I cannot imagine how it will feel when Ruth will no longer be among us."

Emma wiped a tear from her eye. "She is a woman, Samuel. It is the destiny of a woman to leave one house for another. She must leave the loving care of her parents so that she can shower her affection on a new family. She will discover the hidden love of a caring husband and the joy of motherhood. The joys of marriage are many. Watching your child's first smile and knowing that it was conceived from your womb. Growing up along with your child and teaching her and learning as well. She must leave us in order to experience all of this."

"I know Emma, but still … we bring her up, teach her values, shelter her, and then she leaves. Why?"

Emma rested her head on Samuel's shoulder. "If my father had thought the same way, I wouldn't have become your wife."

Samuel didn't say anything more for a few moments, but he squeezed her hand. Emma knew that her logic was right. He finally nodded. "You are right, Emma, as always, but it is so tough."

"We lose what we cling tightly to. Let go and let God."

* * * *

Let go and let God.

Samuel thought about Emma's words. He was full of gratitude toward her. There had been many instances during their marriage when Emma had shown great insight into a problem that had been consuming him. This was another one of them. He sometimes felt that she was more intelligent than he was. She had been his rock in times of tribulation. He now understood what he had been struggling against. He had thought that his battles were his alone. That was not the case. God was on his side, watching him, throwing him a challenge to see how he would face it. Who was he to deny God's designs?

Let God decide what is best for Ruth.

Samuel immediately felt more relaxed. He turned to Emma and smiled. He saw a look of understanding in her eyes as she smiled back.

The children's voices were closer now. Samuel looked toward the barn and saw that they were returning to the house. He observed Ruth, seeing her now in the light of her status as a young lady, instead of the child he had always thought her to be. Yes, she had turned into a fine young woman. Responsible, caring, and intelligent, just like her mother.

He called out to her. "Ruth, my dear, come here."

"Coming, Father" she replied. He watched her stop to instruct her siblings. "Wash your hands and feet. They should be clean."

Then she approached him. "Yes, Father? Do you need dinner?"

Samuel smiled on realizing that Ruth's first concern was about his dinner. Emma had always put family before self, and now Ruth was following in her footsteps. He hugged her. "No, no. I just realized how much you mean to me."

Ruth smiled and hugged her father even more tightly. "When you hug me, I realize how much *you* mean to *me*."

Emma spoke then. "Ruth, your father has something important to discuss with you."

Samuel cleared his throat. "Your mother has informed me that you are aware of your upcoming *rumspringa*. I want to know if you have any questions."

"No, Father. I have no questions. In fact, I am excited to have the opportunity to become a member of the church."

"And you understand that eventually you will marry one of the young men of our community?"

Ruth lowered her eyes. "Yes, Father, I know."

Samuel saw Ruth's eyes moisten. He understood that, like him, she wanted to remain with her family. *It's tougher for her than it is for me*, he thought. *I will lose only Ruth in marriage, but she will be leaving her entire family behind and will be living among new people. What is a father's worry compared to a daughter's?*

He patted her gently. "I know what you are thinking of."

She clung to her father, crying. "I don't want to leave you, Father."

"Don't cry, my dear," he told her. "I won't be marrying you off immediately. You are with us for now. I am sure *Gott* has good things planned for you."

"Yes, Father. I will pray to our Lord to

give me strength." She wiped her tears. "Let me get you some dinner. You must be tired."

Samuel watched her go toward the kitchen. *Yes. She has turned into a mature young lady.* She would be a blessing to the family into which she married. He prayed to God for Ruth's happiness. He would let destiny take its course. *It's Gottes Willes.*

* * * *

Chapter 3

It was early dawn, but Ruth was already awake. She had woken up earlier than usual. She had been so excited that it had been hard for her to go to sleep the night before. Finally the day of *rumspringa* had arrived. She would be going to visit *Ant* Sadie and spend a few days with her.

Ruth did her morning chores more quickly than usual. She milked the cows and helped her mother with the breakfast. When she was done, she collected a few of her clothes and packed them in a small sack. She adjusted her prayer *kapp* and ensured that she looked prim.

Ant Sadie lived a few miles away. It was an hour's walk. The entire family gathered together when it was finally time for Ruth to leave.

"I can come with you, Ruth," Her father offered.

"Thanks, Father, but it's a short journey and I can manage. You have to go to the barn anyway. I will be all right."

Her mother beckoned. "Come here, dear." She gave Ruth a hug, holding her just a little longer than was needed.

"May God be with you," she said.

Ruth ruffled Abram's hair and patted Mary. Mary said, "You have to promise me, *Schweschder*, that you will tell me everything once you come back."

Ruth laughed. "Yes, Mary. I will tell you everything that happens."

Mary beamed. "Goodbye, Sister."

Ruth waved good-bye. Then she turned toward the road and headed to her aunt's house. It was a clear day with blue skies. The morning sun was gentle on her face. Her neighbors waved at her as she passed. They were aware that she would be going to her aunt's house. She waved in reply.

As Ruth crossed a small bridge over a stream that marked the village boundary, she thought, *All right, I am now in a foreign land.* She felt both excited and a little nervous. She had been to her aunt's house only a couple of times before, and this was the first time she had traveled there alone. Her father had been with her on the previous two occasions. Ruth met a few of the villagers along the way, and they nodded at her and smiled.

It was a little over an hour before she saw *Ant* Sadie's cottage. Fields surrounded the small house. She saw her aunt out digging potatoes in the field and called out to her. Sadie smiled broadly.

"Ruth. Oh my, you have changed a lot. You were but a child when I saw you three years back. You are now a lovely young woman. Come. Let me show you inside the house."

They entered the cottage. It was spartan, with only the essentials. Sadie showed Ruth to her room.

"You must be tired. Let me get you some food and milk."

"Thanks, Sadie. That is very kind of you. But let me help you," Ruth said.

"No, you can relax," Sadie told her. "It will take only a couple of minutes."

"Please, I insist."

Sadie smiled. "All right. If you want to help, you can help me by going to the Schrocks' place next door. I need some beans."

"Sure," Ruth agreed. "I will."

Ruth had met Mrs. Schrock once before. She knocked on the door, but there was no response. She looked around and spotted a young man pulling water from a well. His back was turned to her.

"Pardon me, Mr. Schrock," she called.

The man didn't seem to hear her. She walked toward him.

"Mr. Schrock, I needed some beans."

The young man turned toward Ruth, and her heart skipped a beat as she saw the mustached face.

* * * *

Chapter 4

They stared at each other as if in a trance. The man was the first to break out of it. "I'm sorry; I am not a member of the Schrock family. My name is James Townsend. I am living as a tenant here."

"Oh!" Ruth exclaimed. She heard a voice behind her and turned. It was Mrs. Schrock. She hadn't changed a bit from the last time Ruth had seen her.

"Do you need something, child?" Ruth

saw a flicker of recognition in her eyes. "Ruth, is that you?"

Ruth nodded.

"I wouldn't have recognized you, but for your eyes. When did you arrive?"

"Just now. I am on my *rumspringa*."

"Isn't that wonderful? Come inside. We have a lot to talk about."

"I would love to stay, but I have to get back. My *Ant* sent me over to get some beans. I am helping her cook."

"Oh, sure. Give me a moment. I collected a few of them yesterday. By the way, this is Mr. Townsend. He's staying in the farm shed for a few weeks. Mr. Townsend, this is Miss Byler."

James inclined his head. "It's a pleasure to meet you, Miss Byler."

Mrs. Schrock headed into the house to find the beans, leaving Ruth alone with the young man. She wondered what she should say to him.

"So, are you staying with your aunt?" he ventured.

Ruth nodded. "Yes, I come here now and then. How about you?"

"This is the first time I have been to this village. I am a doctor. I'm here to do some research." He smiled at her and she felt her heart flutter.

"You are a doctor?"

"Yes."

"I know a little bit about medicines. My uncle ran an apothecary and I used to help him."

"If you are interested in medicine, I could

probably teach you a few things. I have a lot of medical equipment with me. I'd be happy to show it to you some time if you like."

Ruth realized that she was really attracted to the young man. And now that he had mentioned that he was a doctor, her respect increased. Doctors were life-givers.

"I would like to take a look, but I have to help my aunt with lunch."

"That's fine. You can visit me any time you want. How would after lunch suit you?"

"Er, I am not sure," Ruth hesitated. "I will first have to call upon Mrs. Schrock."

"I understand."

Just then, Mrs. Schrock hailed her from the doorway of her home. "Ruth, here's your beans. Boil them on a slow flame and they will taste delicious. And don't forget to come over to my house later so we can catch up."

Ruth assured her that she would be coming soon. Then she collected the beans and returned to her aunt's cottage. A few minutes later, lunch was ready. They had a delightful lunch, which was coupled with a heartfelt conversation between Ruth and Sadie. They had a lot of catching up to do with one another's lives, and they spent the next few hours discussing everything that had happened since they last met.

* * * *

The next morning, Ruth was up and about early, and she helped Sadie with the daily chores. Sadie was pleased with Ruth's independence and responsibility. Ruth didn't want to be a burden on Sadie and had already decided that she would help her as much as she could.

After breakfast was done, Ruth asked if she could pay a courtesy call to Mrs. Schrock. Sadie agreed and told Ruth not to worry about preparing lunch. Ruth promised to return soon.

As she walked over to the neighboring house, she saw James in the yard. He was feeding oats to the horse.

"Good morning, Mr. Townsend."

James turned around. "Ah, Miss Byler. It is indeed a beautiful morning."

Ruth watched him feed the horse. "The horse seems to like you," she observed.

"Yes. The feeling is mutual." He glanced at Ruth and then continued. "You don't get to see many horses in the city. Initially, I was afraid of him, but now we get along well."

Ruth said, "Horses are similar to people.

They take time to forge a friendship. A stranger that you come to know well is no longer a stranger."

James smiled. "That's true. So, do you have a couple of minutes to spare? I can show you some of the stuff that I am working on."

Ruth thought about it. She had come to visit Mrs. Schrock. However, she found the warm voice of the *Englischer* inexplicably appealing. She wanted to know more about him and what he was doing in their village. *This should only take a few minutes*, she thought. *Mrs. Schrock won't mind a little delay.*

"Please lead the way, Mr. Townsend."

They went to a shed at one corner of the farm. It was larger than she expected on the inside, primarily because it was mostly empty. An old and broken down buggy was kept at one corner. There was a kettle, some bowls, and a few spoons on a table to one side. However, what caught Ruth's attention first was a crate full of books and a pile of scientific equipment, including a microscope, a stethoscope, test tubes, and some medicinal supplies.

"What are those?" she asked, pointing to the modern equipment. Ruth had never seen anything like it before.

"This is my portable laboratory. Here, let me show you."

James showed Ruth the medicines that could cure various diseases. He told her about the microscope that could show you things that could not be seen with the naked eye. Ruth was intrigued, so he showed her what a potato peel looked liked under the microscope. Ruth was impressed. It felt like magic to her.

There was a knock on the door. James opened it to find Mrs. Schrock on the other side.

"Mr. Townsend, did you get a chance to look at the buggy?" Mrs. Schrock inquired.

"Yes. I think it can be fixed. It will take me a couple of days to get it working. I was telling Miss Byler about my work. I apologize if I have distracted her from the purpose for which she came."

"*Ach*, Ruth! I didn't know you were on the premises," Mrs. Schrock said.

"I am sorry, Mrs. Schrock. I was about to call on you."

"It's all right, my child. Take your time."

"No, I think we are done here," Ruth said, glancing at James.

He nodded. "That's right. Feel free to visit

me again sometime. I'd be happy to show you more of the equipment."

"Thank you for your offer," Ruth told him. "I will take my leave now, Mr. Townsend. Have a good day."

"You too," he replied. "Have a good day, Miss Byler."

* * * *

Chapter 5

It had been an eventful day.

Ruth, who had a set routine at home, felt good about herself as she cooked the evening meal. She had thoroughly enjoyed her conversation with Mrs. Schrock. However, she couldn't take her mind off her meeting with James.

He had been a real gentleman and was knowledgeable about his work. She was still astounded by the incredible things she had seen. She felt like he had offered her a peek into the outside world. She wanted to know more about him and his life. She wondered what it would be like to live the life of an *Englischer*. Would it be more exciting than her current life? She wondered what would happen if she decided to live outside of the community in the *Englisch* world.

Sadie spoke. "Ruth, dear, can you cook the vegetables as well? I think I will lie down and rest. I am not feeling well."

"I am sorry, Sadie," Ruth apologized. "I should have helped you more today."

"That's okay, my child," Sadie told her. "I will be in the bedroom if you need me."

Ruth didn't worry too much about why Sadie felt indisposed. She figured that she must be hungry. Ruth worked efficiently to get dinner ready for her.

Dinner was a quiet affair, compared to the previous day. Sadie listened intently as Ruth told her about her day, speaking only when Ruth asked her a question. After a while, she asked Ruth to close the windows.

"Are you feeling all right, *Ant*?" Ruth asked.

"I am a bit tired. I will be fine."

Ruth took a closer look at her aunt and observed that she was shivering. "Are you sure? You don't look so good."

"I will feel better after I have had some sleep," Sadie told her.

Ruth helped Sadie to her bed and gave her some water to drink. As Sadie rested on the bed, she grasped Ruth's hand. Ruth was astounded at the warmth of her touch. She placed her hand on Sadie's forehead and found that she was feverish.

"You are sick, Sadie. Let me make one of Uncle's home remedies. It will cure you," Ruth told her.

"Don't bother yourself, Ruth. I will feel better tomorrow," her aunt said.

"It will take only a couple of minutes. Please, I insist."

Ruth went to the kitchen and gathered the necessary ingredients. A couple of minutes later she was at Sadie's side with the medicinal drink. Sadie drank it and lay back on the bed.

Ruth fanned Sadie's face with her handkerchief. She waited for a few minutes and then touched Sadie's forehead. The fever hadn't subsided.

"Pray for me dear," Sadie said in a weak voice.

So Ruth prayed. She prayed in a soulful and heartfelt voice to God. She prayed that Sadie would be well soon, so that she could have many more conversations with her. She prayed for God to make her strong, hale, and hearty.

Ruth stopped praying on hearing the retching sound.

"*Mein Gott*, help us." She saw that Sadie's face had become bloodless. The medicine wasn't working. Night had fallen. The local apothecary would be closed. No one would help them.

Ruth felt helpless and alone. Sadie's fever could worsen if she waited until morning. Ruth prayed to God for deliverance.

Suddenly, Ruth was struck by an inspiration. *The Englischer* next door! He could help.

Ruth ran barefoot across the field and knocked on the shed door, hoping that James was not asleep. She looked closely and saw a tiny crack of light around the doorframe.

There was a shuffling sound inside and the door opened. James took one look at Ruth and asked, "Is everything all right?"

"My aunt is sick. Can you help me?"

"Sure." He grabbed a coat and followed her.

Back at the house, Ruth led James over to where Sadie rested. He made a quick examination and then told Ruth, "I will be back in a minute. I need to get some of my stuff."

He returned in a few minutes, carrying a stethoscope, a vial of medicine, and a syringe. He checked Sadie's vitals and then gave her an injection.

Ruth watched Sadie anxiously. Sadie looked visibly more relaxed after being injected with the medicine. A few minutes later she was asleep.

James said, "She will feel better in the morning. A good sleep will be very beneficial. I will come back tomorrow morning to check up on her."

Ruth clasped her hands in gratitude. "Thank you so much for helping me. You are a godsend. I don't know what I would have done tonight, if you hadn't come."

"That's okay," James told her. "I didn't do anything special. It was God's will that I was in the neighborhood."

"Yes. God bless you."

"Thank you. I will take my leave now. Goodnight."

* * * *

Chapter 6

By morning, Sadie felt significantly better. Ruth told her about the events of the previous night and Sadie said that the least they could do was to invite James over for lunch. Ruth agreed.

Presently, James came over to check on Sadie. He declared her much improved and admired her for the strength of will that had allowed her to pass through the difficult phase.

Ruth was full of appreciation for what James had done. James was modest about it. He knew he had only done what any doctor would have done. They invited him to join them for lunch. James told her that he would be delighted to have lunch with them, but he was fixing Mrs. Schrock's buggy and would possibly not have time that day. After much cajoling, he agreed to lunch the following day.

The next day, Sadie and Ruth enthusiastically prepared lunch for James. They selected the finest vegetables and fruits and exceeded themselves in ensuring that James would have a delightful and memorable lunch. While they ate their lunch, the three of them indulged in small talk, but it soon became evident to Sadie that James and Ruth were really interested in one another. They swapped stories from their childhoods, comparing their very different experiences. James was keenly interested in how they lived without technology, whereas Ruth wanted to know all about the modern world.

After the lunch was finished and the

dishes were washed, James beckoned Ruth. "Come, I want to show you something."

"What?"

"I'm not going to tell you. You will have to see it for yourself. It's not very far."

Ruth followed him outside, where he led her to the shed. He didn't go inside this time, but instead pointed to the newly painted buggy, which was adjacent to the building. It looked as good as new.

"This is wonderful," Ruth exclaimed.

"Isn't it? Mrs. Schrock hasn't returned yet, but I think she will be delighted when she sees it."

"But does it work?" Ruth asked. "I hope you haven't just pieced it together."

"It will work exactly like it was working

before. How about we take it for a test ride?"

"A ride?"

"Yes. Do you know about the lake? It's only about a mile from here."

"No."

"It's the most beautiful place on earth."

"You don't say."

"Sure, I do. Come with me. I will show you."

* * * *

Sadie watched James hitch his horse to the buggy. When he was finished he opened the buggy door for Ruth and she climbed inside. James lifted the reins and they drove off toward the lake. She could hear them talking from a distance. She was grateful to James for saving her life. However, as an Englischer, his attention to Ruth was improper.

Sadie hoped that Ruth would realize where this was going. She considered her options. James, while certainly a nice guy, was still an outsider. She thought of Samuel. Samuel would expect Sadie to rein Ruth in, in such a situation. Still, after all that he had done for her, Sadie did not wish to hurt his feelings.

I will write to Samuel if they spend time together again tomorrow, she thought.

* * * *

It was late afternoon when Ruth returned. She bustled into the cottage, glowing with enthusiasm.

"Sadie, do you know about the lake over at the western valley?" she asked.

Sadie smiled. "Yes, I do. It is a lovely

place."

"I just visited there with Mr. Townsend. It is so beautiful. Words cannot describe it. The surroundings are lush green and the environment is so serene that you can hear your own breathing."

"I have been there quite a few times" Sadie told her. "It's a place where you feel one with God."

"You are right. The stillness made me feel reflective. I was happy that Mr. Townsend didn't speak much. Maybe he understood what I felt. Both of us were wrapped up in our own thoughts. I think he wanted me to experience the tranquility of the place."

At the mention of the *Englischer*, Sadie was reminded again of Samuel. *Samuel wouldn't appreciate Ruth going out alone with an Englischer.*

She coughed politely. "Ruth, my child, I like Mr. Townsend and I am very thankful for what he did for me the other day. However, I think it's improper for ladies in our community to be going for rides with outsiders."

Sadie saw the enthusiasm drain from Ruth's face. Ruth stared at the fireplace for a long time. Finally she spoke. "You are right, *Ant*. I am here for my *rumspringa*. I should be reflecting upon my future. I don't think I have given it as much thought as I was supposed to. I have been a wayward child."

"Now Ruth, don't blame yourself. You are young in the ways of the world. You are living with me, and it is now my responsibility to take care of you. I only want to ensure that you follow the right path."

Ruth felt guilty. She had come here on her own because her parents trusted her. Yet she felt a growing emotion for the *Englischer*. It was an emotion that she was afraid to name because she wasn't sure she would be able to quell her emotions, once she admitted them. She was reluctant to probe too deeply because she dreaded what she would find.

Dear God, help me. You have given me a tough test. Please also give me the strength to do the right thing.

After reposing in her faith in God for a few minutes, Ruth felt calmer. She clasped Sadie's hand. "I apologize, Sadie. I will act in an appropriate manner the next time."

"I am sure you will, dear."

Despite her words, however, Ruth was still thinking of the mustached *Englischer* when she went to bed. She was a little annoyed that James was still on her mind. She knew that Sadie was right. It wasn't proper for her to continue to spend time with him. She decided she would try to keep a low profile for the next few days.

* * * *

In the shed across the yard, James was wide awake. In times past he would have opened a bottle of wine to help lull him to sleep. Yet things had been different for the past few days. He hadn't had a drop of drink since he had met Ruth.

James looked at the locked suitcase in the corner. It contained two bottles of the finest white wine. He was tempted, but with some willpower he turned his gaze away. He focused his mind on the simple life of the Amish community. They led such pure lives. He was fascinated by them. Especially Ruth. He had fallen for her the first time he saw her in the village marketplace. It had been a surprise when she turned up as his neighbor. He felt as if fate was on his side. Today had been really special.

He had enjoyed spending time with her, both at lunch and later at the lake.

Yet, a thought kept gnawing at him.

What are you trying to prove? She is a lady of the Amish. There is no future in this relationship.

His logical mind told him what he didn't want to hear. Yet his heart had a different logic. *Love conquers all. She will love me despite who I am. I will show her my positive side.*

She is pure like the wind-driven snow, his mind retorted. *You have a drinking problem. Why would she accept you?*

He sighed. He knew that this was the reason he hadn't had a drink for the past few days. He wanted to prove to himself that he could reform.

James glanced at the locked suitcase again. The temptation was still there. He knew that a cup would help him to deal with the pain of his internal struggle. With some difficulty he pulled his gaze away.

* * * *

Chapter 7

"Good morning, Miss Byler."

Ruth was startled. She had been picking radishes for their lunch and hadn't noticed James approaching. She turned to find him standing next to her, a kindly smile on his face. She remembered her discussion with Sadie yesterday. She was unsure how to respond to his attention.

"Good morning, Mr. Townsend," she somehow managed.

"How is your aunt doing?"

"Much better. I would say she is completely recovered." Ruth realized she couldn't avoid answering his questions. It would seem rude.

"Can I see her?" he asked.

Ruth acquiesced. It was better if they didn't spend time alone, she knew. She called out to her aunt. Sadie came outside and smiled at James. "Good morning, Mr. Townsend."

"How are you doing, ma'am?" James asked.

"I am feeling good. And it's all thanks to you."

"It was nothing. I just did what any doctor would have done."

"You are too kind," she told him.

After a brief pause, James turned to Ruth.

"Miss Byler, would you do me the pleasure of joining me again today for an expedition to the lake?"

Ruth turned crimson. "I'm sorry, Mr. Townsend, but Sadie and I will be knitting together this afternoon," she told him.

"Oh! Maybe later then." He waited for an answer, but Ruth didn't say anything more. Finally, James continued, "I will take my leave now. Mrs. Schrock has given me a few chores to do."

* * * *

Sadie watched James leave. It was good that they had made plans to knit today. Otherwise, it would have been difficult for Ruth to decline his request. Sadie became even more determined to let Samuel know what was happening. He would be able to guide her.

She went inside and immediately

composed a short letter. She would post the letter that afternoon. She hoped that Samuel would receive it by the following day and be able to assist her in this dilemma.

* * * *

Chapter 8

Samuel received the letter the following afternoon. He felt distraught at Sadie's words. A myriad of thoughts went through his mind. His worst fears had been realized. Ruth and an *Englischer*...

"You seem to be ill at ease, Samuel. Is everything all right?" Emma asked, concerned.

Samuel didn't reply. Instead, he handed her the letter.

After reading it, she asked, "What are we going to do?"

Samuel's jaw was set. "I know what *I* am

going to do. I will go there first thing in the morning and bring Ruth back."

"But … the *rumspringa*. You know we need to let her complete it."

Samuel shook his head. "No, I think it's better for everyone if she comes back."

Emma closed her eyes and started to pray. Samuel watched her lips move softly in devotion. He closed his own eyes and prayed to God for guidance.

Emma's words from the other day came back to him. *You lose what you cling tightly to.*

Samuel considered this for a minute. *Was he being too protective of Ruth?* She was no longer a child. She was now a young woman who could make her own decisions. Wasn't that the very point of *rumspringa*? She needed to have the opportunity to choose for herself.

He thought of the *Englischer*. He was showing an undue and improper interest in his child. He knew that someone should draw the line on that. It wasn't good for Ruth to be influenced by an outsider.

Samuel looked at Emma. She had opened her eyes and was now watching him closely, trying to read his thoughts. Samuel smiled.

"I have decided to bring Ruth back."

Emma nodded silently. "I will get your things ready in the morning."

* * * *

Samuel didn't sleep well. He tossed and turned for most of the night. He prayed again to God. He felt better after leaving his cares with the Almighty. It was after midnight when he finally fell asleep. He woke up feeling much more relaxed than he had the night before. He didn't need to confront the *Englischer*. He would simply bring Ruth home.

He got into his buggy and took the lunch pail that Emma had packed for him. He smiled at her. "Everything will be alright."

"Yes. I know that God will make everything all right," she told him.

Samuel was struck the simple trust Emma had in God. He wondered if he was as trusting of God as she was. He absentmindedly slapped the reins. The horse started forward, but Samuel was still lost in his thoughts. They crossed the village and the buggy ambled along through the open fields. It was a bright sunny day. He loosened the reins and continued to ponder Emma's faith in God. Her words came back to him: *Let go and let God.*

What was he so worried about, he wondered? He had always felt God's presence in his life. Today, as his buggy meandered through the green fields, he felt God's presence more strongly than ever before. *God is on my side. Why should I worry about anything?*

He stopped the buggy and turned it around. He no longer felt the need to watch over Ruth. A greater power was already watching over her. A few minutes later he was back at the farm.

"Samuel, you are back?" Emma asked.

"Yes ... you know, er, I thought ..." Samuel stumbled for words.

Emma smiled and embraced him. "You did the right thing."

* * * *

Sadie received Samuel's note that afternoon. It was brief and to the point.

Ruth will be all right. God is watching over

her.

Sadie smiled. This was indeed the case. Sadie had never doubted her faith and now, with Samuel's note, she felt reassured. She no longer worried about how Ruth would avoid the *Englischer's* attentions. She knew that it didn't matter. In the end, everything would be resolved as it should be.

The next few days were quiet. Surprisingly, James didn't pay them a visit. Sadie was grateful, but wondered about the turn of events. It wasn't as if he wasn't in his shed. She intermittently saw him coming and going from the farm.

A chat with Mrs. Schrock revealed that James was busy with his research and had been quite reclusive recently.

Sadie shared this with Ruth and saw her

visibly relax. Ruth had been thinking a lot about the choice she would be making. She had talked with Sadie at length about becoming a member of the church. Sadie had advised Ruth to pray at the church service the next day.

The church service was being held at a Mrs. Yoder's house. There were only a few people there. As the service started, Ruth thought about how her *rumspringa* had gone so far, and the choice that she had to make. She thought about her family, her friends, Sadie, and even James. She asked God to bless everyone whom she had met in her life. She felt good after the prayer was concluded.

When the service was over, Sadie said, "Come, let me introduce you to our host."

She led Ruth over to Mrs. Yoder. "Good morning, Rebecca. How are you? This is my niece, Ruth."

Mrs. Yoder nodded happily. "Welcome. I don't think we have met before."

Ruth said, "No, we haven't. I am here on my *rumspringa*."

Mrs. Yoder smiled. "Ah, *rumspringa*. Do you know that is the toughest part of life?"

Ruth was puzzled. She had never thought of it that way. "I would have thought that managing a husband and children after marriage would be tougher. Why do you think this?"

"Few people realize that *rumspringa* is a test," Mrs. Yoder told her. "The *Ordnung* knows it, which is why *rumspringa* is the gateway to becoming a church member."

"I don't understand. Why do you call it a test?"

"*Rumspringa* is a test of your ability to

resist temptation. Have you felt as if you were at a crossroad, one path leading you to the church, the other leading you out of the community?"

Ruth mulled this over. When she had met James, she had unconsciously considered both options. Mrs. Yoder was right. *Rumspringa* was about temptation and making choices. She nodded. "I have been a victim of temptation."

Mrs. Yoder quoted the Bible: "No temptation has overtaken you except what is common to mankind. And God is faithful; He will not let you be tempted beyond what you can bear. But when you are tempted, He will also provide a way out so that you can endure it."

* * * *

The days passed quickly for Ruth and Sadie, and it was soon time for Ruth to return to her family. Sadie assisted Ruth with her packing.

She gave her some of her treasured fruits from the backyard. "Take these. Share them with Abram and Mary. It's been a long time since I have seen those kids. Give them my love and blessings."

"Of course, Sadie. I will pass on your message."

"I know you will."

"I think I should pay a visit to Mrs. Schrock before I leave," Ruth said. "She has been very kind to me."

"Yes," Sadie agreed. "You should let her know that you are leaving."

Ruth walked over to Mrs. Schrock's house and knocked on the door. Mrs. Schrock opened the door and beamed at Ruth.

"Ruth, how are you? Come inside."

As she entered, Ruth said, "Mrs. Schrock, I wanted to thank you for your hospitality these past few days. I also wanted to let you know that I am returning home to my family."

"*Ach!* That's a pity. When are you leaving?" Mrs. Schrock asked her.

"I will be leaving in an hour."

"I will not let you leave without tasting some of my breakfast."

Ruth smiled. She had already finished her breakfast, but she knew that Mrs. Schrock would insist that she eat with her.

"I will have just a little bite."

They sat down to have a chat. Ruth told Mrs. Schrock about her *rumspringa* and her decision to become a church member. Mrs. Schrock told her about the time when she was a young woman on her *rumspringa*. She had been a rebel during her youth and she and her brother had almost decided to leave the community. However, better sense had prevailed. Ruth listened to her story with interest.

After breakfast was over, the two of them sat on the front porch. Ruth could see James's shed from where she sat. She briefly felt as if someone was watching her from the window, but the sensation lasted only an instant. She looked closely but she couldn't see anyone. Ruth thought about James. It had been a long time since they had talked. She had thought about him several times over the past few days and had wondered why he hadn't visited her anymore. She wondered if she would miss the *Englischer*. He had been a really nice gentleman.

The thought of James brought a flush to her face. The emotions that she had suppressed came back to her. She felt an unexpected desire to see him, even if it was for the last time. His handsome features filled her mind.

Mrs. Schrock's words broke into her reverie. "Ruth, do me a favor. Can you go over to Mr. Townsend's room and ask him to come see me? The buggy is making grinding noises and I hope he can fix it."

Ruth's eyes snapped open. "Me?"

"Yes, please be a dear and beckon Mr. Townsend over here."

Ruth's cheeks flushed. She didn't want Mrs. Schrock to see her reluctance and then have to explain why she wanted to avoid James. After a moment's hesitation, she acquiesced. "Yes, Mrs. Schrock. I will inform him."

She walked over to the shed, her heart beating more loudly with each step she took. The door was closed. Maybe he wasn't inside.

Hope swelled up inside her. She wasn't sure in her heart whether she wanted to see him or not.

She tentatively knocked on the door.

There was no sound from the inside. She waited a few moments and knocked again.

She heard the sound of dragging feet, followed by a scraping and then a tinkling noise. The bolts slid open and her heart leapt as she saw James in the flesh.

* * * *

Chapter 9

"Good morning, Miss Byler. How are you doing?"

The warm voice and the handsome face brought Ruth's emotions to the fore. She blushed as she remembered the time they had spent together, happy in each other's company. He had been different from the young men of their community, and that had made him attractive to her. Now, seeing him again after so many days, she realized that she had missed him more than she would have cared to admit.

"Would you like to come in?" he asked.

Ruth realized that she hadn't answered his first question. "I'm sorry. Mrs. Schrock wanted you to check the buggy."

"I will look into it presently." He glanced at her.

Ruth looked at his eyes and realized that there was something amiss. She listened to him talk and then observed that while his words were friendly, his eyes were remote. And his diction was slow and at times indistinct.

"Come over here. We can sit at the table," James said in a slurred voice.

And it was then that she saw it.

Ruth stopped in her tracks and looked at the bottle of white wine atop the table. "You drink spirits?" She asked in an incredulous voice.

He picked up the bottle with a shaking hand. "I drink alcohol every day."

Ruth realized suddenly that James was drunk. She backed toward the door. "Excuse me, I need some fresh air."

James sat down heavily on the table. "Whatever. Come back soon."

Ruth opened the door and bolted.

* * * *

James got up and looked out of the window. He saw Ruth walking back to her aunt's house. *It's for her own good,* he thought. He smiled sadly and thought, *it's for my own good too.*

He walked back to the table and picked up the wine bottle with a steady hand, his ruse finished. He waited for the temptation to come. It didn't. He felt only a sense of loss.

His mind had tussled with his heart for many days, but he was a man of science and eventually the logical mind had triumphed. James had realized that there was nothing to be gained by falling in love with an Amish girl. Their two worlds were just too far apart, and they didn't have a future together. He had decided to avoid contact with Ruth.

It had gone well. James had thrown himself wholeheartedly into his work. That had helped to keep him from thinking about her. His only worry was that Ruth herself might be attracted to him and might approach him. If she did he feared his resolve would not be strong enough to keep him from saying or doing something he would regret. He had eventually come up with a solution for that as well. He would act as if he were drunk. He had executed his part perfectly today.

James glanced again at the bottle. He hadn't drunk a drop for many days now. He knew why he had abstained. He wondered if there was a reason now to continue. Ruth would not come back. He might as well drink. Yet the desire to drink was absent. He took the bottle, placed it back in the suitcase, and locked it.

There was only one thought in his mind.

I will try to be pure and simple like the Amish.

* * * *

Ruth had been walking for an hour when she saw the familiar house set amidst a green farm.

Home! Finally!

Her pace quickened as home beckoned her. Abram saw her from afar and shouted loudly, "*Schweschder* is back. She has returned."

Ruth laughed and sprinted toward Abram. Abram ran across the field to meet her and held her tightly. "We all missed you, *Schweschder*."

Ruth looked up to see the rest of the family gathered in the doorway. Tears of joy streamed down her face. "I also missed you all."

* * * *

Chapter 10

"Father, I need to talk with you about something," Ruth said in a quiet voice.

It was evening and they had just finished dinner. Ruth was happy to be back. It was incredible how comfortable everything felt when you were at home. She had spent most of the day talking about what she and Sadie had done during her *rumspringa*.

"Sure dear, is there anything that is bothering you?" Samuel asked.

"No. I'm fine. I just felt like I needed to share something with you. I met an *Englischer* when I was at *Ant* Sadie's house." Ruth paused and looked at her father to see if he would say anything, but her father simply nodded and gestured at her to carry on.

"*Ant* Sadie fell sick one day. The *Englischer* was a doctor, and he helped to cure her sickness."

"That was really gracious of him."

"Yes. We were grateful for what he had done. He ... er ... became interested in me."

"Indeed?"

Ruth lowered her eyes. "And at one point, I even felt that I liked him."

Samuel raised an eyebrow. "And?"

Ruth continued hastily, "But later I realized that he was not the right choice for me, so I avoided seeing him. I wanted to share this because I felt guilty about it. I don't want to hide anything from you. But I feel that I acted immaturely. You might think of me as a bad child. I am sorry." Tears trickled down Ruth's face as she confessed the thing that had been gnawing at her.

Samuel reached out and put a hand on her shoulder. "Ruth, why do you think of yourself as a bad child? You are my good daughter and you did what was right."

"I did? I don't think so." Ruth was still

crying.

"Yes, you did the right thing," Samuel emphasized. "Your values determined the choice you made. You weren't led astray. I am proud of you. You are a good example of a young Amish woman in the community."

Ruth wiped her eyes, thinking about what her father had said.

Samuel continued, "God brought you into the world. He gave you a family, food, friends, and a good life. You are God's creation. How can a child of God be bad? God is always watching over you. He is guiding you on the right path. And look, in the end, you realized that the outsider was not meant for you. That was God's will."

Ruth nodded her head. It was indeed God's will. She closed her eyes and started praying. She prayed to God that His benevolence would always be upon her. She asked for wisdom to distinguish right from wrong. She prayed for a loving soul mate that would understand her needs and provide for them, and she promised God she would be a worthy wife, a caring mother, and a respectable woman of the community.

Ruth felt relaxed and lighter after her prayer. She felt as if God had listened to her prayer and would grant her what she had asked. She opened her eyes and saw her father looking at her. She smiled. "Thank you, Father, for listening. You have always been so supportive."

"Age gives one wisdom," he replied. "Would do you me a favor, child?"

"Yes, Father. What do you want?"

"When you are my age, remember to give

your own child the same wisdom and support."

Ruth thought about it. "Yes, Father."

"Now go sleep. It's been a long day for you."

"Yes, Father. Good night."

Ruth laid herself on the bed and thought again of the events of the day. She thought about God's plans for her. She prayed again and fell asleep with God's name on her lips.

In her dream, Ruth saw a handsome young man with golden hair. He wore a straw hat and had a dazzling smile. The young man invited her to take a ride in his buggy. Her smile mirrored his as she accepted the invitation. They chatted and laughed together. They had eyes only for each other.

The handsome young man finally spoke

the words Ruth had been yearning to hear. "There comes a time in a young man's life when he desires to be united in marriage to a fine woman." The young man looked at her. "You are a fine young woman, Ruth." Ruth felt her cheeks burning and her heart beating fast.

She opened her eyes.

It was the first light of morning. She closed her eyes again, hoping to revisit the dream. She wanted to know if she had accepted the proposal. But the dream had slipped away. She opened her eyes and sat up. She smiled as she thought about the dream.

God has a plan for me.

* * End Of Part I* *

2. GOD HAS A PLAN FOR YOU

Chapter 1

Jacob Miller stormed out of his uncle's house.

He clenched his fists and walked at a fast pace. How could his Uncle be so calm after everything that had happened?

Jacob was so engrossed in his thoughts that he didn't notice the approaching young lady and bumped right into her, knocking her to the ground.

He bent down to assist her, concerned that she may have hurt herself. Jacob was immediately struck by the simple beauty of her face. Her auburn hair was tied in a knot, and the hazel eyes looked wonderingly at him.

"My apologies, ma'am. I was lost in my thoughts," Jacob sputtered.

She took the proffered hand, and got to her feet. She smiled and it was like the first bloom of spring washing away his worries.

She said, "That makes two of us. Even I wasn't watching where I was going."

Jacob smiled, happy to see that she wasn't hurt. He was interested in the young lady. "My name is Jacob Miller. What's yours?"

"My name is Ruth Byler. I live yonder." She pointed to her farm. "You seem to be new to the village. Where are you staying?"

"I am staying at my Uncle's house." He pointed to the Miller's house.

"Oh! You are Mr. Miller's nephew?"

"Yes."

"I was going there myself."

Jacob thought of accompanying her, but was reminded of what had just happened. As much as he would have loved to know her more, he knew he couldn't come along with her after the disagreement with his Uncle.

"You carry on. Hope to see you around." He said.

Jacob kept watching Ruth as she walked towards his Uncle's house. For a moment, her presence had made him forget everything that had happened in the past three days. They had been the most painful and saddest days of his life.

* * * *

"Here you are." Mrs. Miller handed over the potatoes to Ruth.

"Thank you, Mrs. Miller." Ruth paused,

wondering whether to broach the subject of Jacob.

"You seem lost, child. Are you all right?"

"I am fine. I just … er … met your nephew."

Mrs. Miller sighed. "He and his brother came in this morning. May *Gott* guide their poor souls."

* * * *

Why?

That was the question Jacob Miller needed the answer to. He had been asking that question for three days now. And he didn't have an answer.

Nobody did.

No one he had asked was able to tell him why. Or if they had, he hadn't accepted their answer. It was *Gott's* will, they had said.

Baloney! He uttered and immediately regretted it. He silently admonished himself for speaking against the will of God.

He could see little puppies playing in the farm that he was passing by. The puppies were dancing around each other, joyous and carefree. The sight of it made him a little happy. There hadn't been much to be happy about recently.

Jacob's father had died three days ago.

The thought of it brought his emotions rushing back. His father had been everything to him. A teacher, mentor and a friend. He had been very proud of his father and had hoped that he would be an upstanding man like his father.

That had been till a few days ago.

With his father gone, all his hopes and aspirations had disappeared. There had been nothing left for him to look forward to. He looked up at the sky. It had turned dark. Ominous gray clouds heralded the imminent advent of rain.

He was such a wonderful person. Why did he leave us so soon? He asked the question to the heavens.

There was no answer.

He hung his head. The tears streamed silently from his eyes. Maybe there were no answers to be found anywhere. He looked around. The puppies had gone. Maybe they had sensed that it was going to rain. Jacob looked up and down the road. There was not a soul in sight. Maybe there was no meaning to life. There didn't seem to be a reason to exist.

The tears ran faster.

A flash of lightning careened across the sky, followed by a resounding crack of thunder. As the rain poured relentlessly over his tear-stricken face, Jacob felt very lonely.

* * * *

Chapter 2

"You did the right thing," Sarah said. "Why do you feel guilty?"

Ruth looked at Sarah and sighed. It was afternoon and the two of them were in Ruth's kitchen. Sarah had come in to find out how Ruth's *rumspringa* had gone. Ruth had arrived from her Aunt's house yesterday. She had promised her friend Sarah that she would share everything that happened during her *rumspringa*.

Ruth had told Sarah about the *Englischer* and how she had eschewed propriety and gone on a buggy ride with him. Ruth had found him decent till she had seen him drinking alcohol, and had abandoned all thought of him.

Sarah tried to convince Ruth, "Nothing

untoward happened between the two of you. You went out only once with him. And in the end, you avoided him and came back home."

Ruth nodded. "I even asked my father to forgive me."

"And?"

"Father forgave me. He said I did the right thing in the end."

Sarah was exasperated. "Well, then why are you burning your heart thus?"

"Because I did the wrong thing, that's why." Ruth was on the verge of tears. "I was so close to abandoning my community. My home, my family, everything, for a stranger." Ruth looked around the familiar kitchen for reassurance and shuddered at the thought of what could have happened.

Sarah couldn't see her best friend unhappy. She patted Ruth's hand. "But dear, nothing of that sort happened."

Ruth clutched at her apron. "I know, but I can't forgive myself for what happened."

Sarah shook her head. "You will have to let go of your past."

"Father told me the same thing. He said that it was *Gott's* will."

"Your father is right. You have been thinking about it too much. It was meant to happen. God allowed it to happen. Put your faith in the Lord and he will show you the path. God has a plan for you."

Ruth dwelled on it. *Indeed. God has a plan.*

"*Schweschder*, come quick." Ruth's brother Abram beckoned at her from the kitchen door.

Ruth was intrigued. Abram's voice was a little too concerned for a ten year old. She followed Abram out of the house with Sarah close behind her.

The afternoon sun was hidden behind the clouds. It had rained a lot and the atmosphere was still chilly. The greenery of the hills spread out everywhere one could look. Small houses dotted the countryside. Ruth saw Abram slow down as he reached a muddy field and stop next to a sleeping animal. Closer, she could see that it was a newborn goat.

Ruth stooped over the baby goat and saw that its eyes were shut. She could see that it was shivering due to the wet and muddy field.

Abram looked at Ruth. His eyes full of questions.

Sarah looked around. "Where is the

mother?"

"I don't know." Abram replied.

Ruth was familiar with all the animals on their large farm. She had been raised with cows, goats, horses and sheep. One look at the kid was enough to convince her that it was unwell.

Sarah came to the same conclusion. "We will have to do something. This baby is sick."

Ruth felt a deep sympathy for the animal. *May* Gott *help this poor kid.* She wondered if the kid's mother had abandoned the baby because it was sick at birth. Ruth stroked the kid's body gently. The animal shuddered. It was barely warm.

Ruth looked around for the goat's mother. "There." She pointed to a fallen mass of branches and ran towards it. Sarah and Abram followed her.

Ruth looked at the mother goat. One of its legs was trapped under a fallen branch. Apparently, the goat had sheltered itself under the tree when it was raining. The branch had snapped and fallen over it.

The three of them carefully lifted the branches. But the goat didn't move. Its leg was bleeding. It tried raising itself but faltered.

Ruth said, "We will carry both mother and kid to our home. We can take care of them at the farm."

Back at the farm, Ruth cleaned the goat's leg and wrapped it with a cotton cloth. The bleeding minimized, but it didn't stop completely. She tied a second cloth around the first. The kid hopped around its mother. It wanted to play.

Ruth smiled inadvertently. It had been

Gott's will for her to find the goat and nurse it back to health. She remembered the time one of the sheep had been drenched by rain due to broken shingles in the barn. The sheep had nearly died due to the cold and rain. *That was a tough time, however Gott was with us. This time also we will persevere.*

* * * *

"Do you want me to make dinner? Ruth asked her mother.

"Thanks," Her mother, Emma Byler said.

"The Millers have guests." Ruth's mind was on her conversation with Mrs. Miller earlier today.

"Yes, I know. It's so sad when young brothers barely out of their teenage years witness their father pass away. I knew Mr. Miller's brother. He had come here once before. Your father and I will visit the brothers and pay our respects."

Ruth's mind went over her encounter with Jacob. He hadn't shown any signs of grief during their brief interaction. Maybe he was reserved and stoic, Ruth thought with pity. She uttered a brief prayer requesting the Lord to give him strength to face his sorrows.

Ruth's mother continued. "I am thinking of inviting them over for dinner. As neighbors, it's the least we can do."

Ruth's heart skipped a beat. "... Dinner?"

"Yes. I am sure they would appreciate it."

Ruth thought of the dream that she had seen. She had bumped into a young man. Today's meeting with Jacob had been remarkably similar to her dream. Her cheeks turned crimson as a new thought struck her.

Is he the one?

Chapter 3

Ruth woke up with the first light of morning and went to the pen to check on the goat and its kid. She was surprised to see that they both were still sleeping. *Maybe they need more rest after what happened yesterday.* She told herself that she will check back on the goat later in the day.

It was going to be a busy day. The Millers were coming over for dinner. She told her mother that they would cook the choicest food. Her mother smiled at Ruth's enthusiasm.

Ruth went out to gather the vegetables. She thought of what Sarah had told her. *God has a plan for you.*

I wonder if Jacob is part of my plan. She

wondered. Ruth was suddenly struck by a thought. *What if Jacob comes to know of the Englischer? Would he still want to be with me?*

Ruth was anguished. The guilt over her *rumspringa* had still not left her.

* * * *

"They're here!" Mary called excitedly.

Ruth looked down at her dress. She straightened the folds on her clothes in an effort to look prim, adjusted her prayer *kapp,* and hoped that she looked presentable. She usually didn't check herself so thoroughly; however, today was different.

She wanted to look good for Jacob.

It had been a rushed couple of hours for Ruth in the kitchen. She had outdone herself with the dinner. Her mother had been pleased with Ruth's zeal.

"You've helped me a lot today. I don't know how I would have prepared the dishes for the guests if not for you and Mary," Ruth's mother said. "But Mrs. Miller won't be joining us. She is not well and excused herself from the invitation."

Ruth heard her father in the drawing room welcoming the guests. Mr. Miller introduced the nephews and the four men sat down to talk. She could hear her father commiserating the loss.

In the meanwhile, Ruth, Mary, and their mother arranged the dishes on the table. They would wait for the men to finish their talk and for the summons for dinner.

It wasn't long in coming. Ruth's father, Samuel asked his guests if they would like to dine. The Millers nodded their heads.

Samuel entered the kitchen. "Emma, is dinner ready?"

"Yes, Samuel," she replied.

"Good." He went out. They heard Samuel say, "Please join me at the dining table."

Samuel came in followed by Mr. Miller and the nephews, Jacob and Isaac. Jacob glanced at Ruth and smiled. Somehow Ruth felt as if he had wanted to see her again. Samuel introduced his wife and children to the guests. Ruth had met Jacob but not his brother, Isaac. Isaac had soft brown eyes that matched his brown hair. He was quiet and didn't speak much. The men settled down and the ladies served them food.

Ruth's father gestured Ruth to serve food to Jacob. Ruth was surprised. She wondered if her father wanted to match her up with Jacob.

Jacob looked up at her as she filled his

plate. Ruth felt conscious and flustered. She tried to focus only on the food, but Jacob's steady gaze was unnerving her.

Emma coughed. "Ruth, please serve everyone."

Ruth looked around. Everyone was looking wonderingly at her. She glanced down and was startled to see that Jacob's plate was full and she had kept on serving food to him. The food was almost about to overflow from the plate. Jacob was still looking at her. He too hadn't noticed.

Samuel tried to divert everyone's attention. "Have the boys completed their *rumspringa*?" He asked Mr. Miller.

"Yes they have. Their mother suggested that the boys come over here so that they can have a change after everything that happened. I would like to take them under my care for a few weeks. If the boys want, they are free to stay here longer, though I need to have a word with the Bishop prior to that."

Samuel agreed. "Yes, staying longer will require the Bishop's permission."

Jacob interrupted. "I am not sure how long I want to stay here."

Isaac patted his brother's shoulder. "Have faith in God. It will be all right."

"No, it won't be all right." Jacob retorted.

Mr. Miller was at a loss for words. The ladies looked at each other.

Samuel said, "Let us focus on the now and not worry about the morrow. Jacob will let us know what he would like to do next. Won't you, Jacob?"

Jacob didn't say anything. The conversation simmered down after that with Mr. Miller reminiscing about his brother.

The dinner was finished an hour later. The guests paid their compliments for the excellent food.

Jacob came up to Ruth. "Thank you for your hospitality tonight. I appreciate it."

"You are welcome." Ruth paused. "I am not sure if you are aware, but we have our community church service tomorrow at our home. Will you be joining us?"

Jacob was quiet for a moment and then simply said, "Good night, Miss Byler."

* * * *

Chapter 4

"The Millers haven't arrived yet." Ruth

was concerned.

"Yes, it is unusual for them to be late to the service," Emma replied while getting the house ready for the church service. Ruth and Mary were helping their mother. The service was to start in a few minutes.

Ruth had wondered about Jacob for most of the night after he had left. He had appeared like a gentleman in their first encounter, but last evening he had been curt to the point of being rude. Ruth wanted to give him the benefit of the doubt. She put down his behavior to his father passing away.

"Looks like they have arrived." Emma said.

"Where?" Ruth craned her neck to see above the throng of people who had come into their home. She could see Mr. and Mrs. Miller.

Isaac was behind them, but Jacob was nowhere to be seen.

The Millers saw them and came to their side. Emma asked, "Where is Jacob?"

"He wanted to be left alone." Isaac said.

Ruth found it odd. She had never heard of anyone who had skipped church service. It was unthinkable. She had thought of him as a decent person during their first meeting, but Jacob's every action after that had been inscrutable.

Mary nudged Ruth and whispered. "The prayer is about to start."

Everyone joined in the prayer. Their collective voices were soulful and deep. Ruth prayed fervently. She prayed for her family, for Isaac and Jacob, and even for the goat and its kid. She expressed her gratitude towards God for the regular opportunity to host the church service. She told herself that she will strive to be a respectful Amish woman.

After the service was completed, the villagers expressed their thanks to Mr. and Mrs. Byler for hosting the service. Emma beckoned Ruth. Ruth was torn between her desire to meet Jacob and the need to help her mother. She decided on the latter.

Ruth helped her mother set the furniture back in place that they had arranged for the church service. She cleaned the tables and swept the floor. After an hour, everything was looking good.

"*Mudder*, can I go over to the Miller's house for a few minutes?" Ruth asked.

"Sure. Do you want anything?" Emma asked.

"No, I just wanted to check on Jacob. He

didn't come in today."

Emma was surprised by Ruth's interest in Jacob, but she didn't object. "Yes, I also wondered why he didn't come today. Let me know what happened."

A few minutes later, Ruth was approaching the Miller's farm. She could see Isaac feeding oats to the horses. She waved to him, "Where is Jacob?"

"He's out at the back." Isaac responded.

Ruth went behind the house and found Jacob playing with the Millers' dog. He held the dog in his arms and was rubbing its body and cooing to it. It was the first time Ruth had seen Jacob showing so much spontaneity. He looked a different person.

Jacob saw Ruth and went over to her. "Good morning, Miss Byler."

Ruth ignored the pleasantries. She was curious to understand his absence. "Why didn't you come to the church service today?"

Ruth watched Jacob's face and felt as if a veil had come over his eyes. He turned away. "I didn't feel like coming."

Ruth gasped. "How can you say such a thing? We pray to God at every service, and God gives us the path to lead our lives. How can you not come to such an important event?"

Jacob winced as if he was in physical pain. He turned to Ruth. "Please, I want to be left alone."

"No, I insist. I need to know why."

"All right. You want to know why. Here's why. I have lost my faith." Jacob walked off in a huff.

Ruth clutched her hand to her mouth. It was too much to absorb. She thought of calling Jacob back, but wasn't sure what she could say that would make him listen. Ruth turned around and found Isaac watching her. Apparently, he had heard their conversation.

Isaac approached her. "I apologize on behalf of my brother, Miss Byler."

"No, it's all right."

Isaac continued. "Jacob was one of the most devout persons in our village. He was very close to God. I don't understand how he has changed so suddenly."

Ruth was surprised on hearing this. She had only met Jacob yesterday. She realized that she didn't know how he was before his father's death. "Has he really changed a lot?"

Isaac said in a forlorn voice, "I feel very

sad for him. Jacob was the most positive and cheerful person you could meet. He used to believe that God guided us on the path of our lives. It was the exact words that you just said to him. Maybe it reminded him of what he once believed in. I have been praying to God to give him wisdom and courage to find his path again." Isaac murmured a quick prayer.

Ruth closed her eyes. A tear escaped down her cheek. She hoped that things would turn out all right for the two brothers. She felt sad for them, but didn't know what to do. Isaac was managing his father's death better than Jacob.

"Is there anything I can do to help?"

"Yes, please pray for Jacob."

"I will." Ruth promised. "Do you think Jacob will ever get back to his former self?"

Isaac said, "I don't know. I think something inside him died with our father's death."

* * * *

"Ruth went over to visit Jacob," Emma told Samuel.

Samuel thought about it. "Jacob's father was a good man. So is his uncle. But I am not sure about that boy."

"Why do you say that?" Emma was curious.

"I initially felt that Jacob would be a good match for Ruth. But now, I am not so sure. Jacob seems to be arrogant and haughty. He comes across more like an *Englischer* than one of us."

"The boy has had a traumatic experience. I would suggest that you hold your judgment for a few days."

Samuel nodded. Jacob's behavior had stymied him. He remembered meeting him a couple of years back, and he had been impressed by the industrious and obedient son. Samuel had made a mental note of Jacob as one of the prospects for his daughter. But Jacob's behavior in the past two days had been completely unlike what he had seen earlier.

Samuel smiled on thinking about Emma's advice. As usual, she had pointed out in her gentle manner his errors. He had been quick to judge Jacob. It would be more prudent to wait and see the path God would unveil to him.

Samuel uttered a prayer requesting God to give him more wisdom.

* * * *

Chapter 5

"No!" Ruth cried.

The kid had pulled and chewed the cotton cloth that was wrapped around the mother goat's leg. The cloth was completely shredded, and the wound was bleeding again. Ruth was annoyed and pushed the kid away. The kid bleated faintly and strayed off. Mary picked up the kid and consoled it. Ruth looked at the mother goat's wound.

"This does not look good. The kid has aggravated the wound." Ruth told Mary.

"Maybe we can keep the kid away from its mother for some time until she recovers." Mary suggested.

Ruth agreed. "Put the kid in the second pen. The goat there has just delivered, and the kid can drink its milk when hungry."

Mary took the kid and went to do as Ruth had advised.

Ruth turned her attention back to the goat. She wasn't sure how long the wound had been open. She started to clean the wound. The goat was weak with the loss of blood. It was lying on its side without making any attempt to wake up. "Get up, Mother Goat. It's time to eat." Ruth called out to the goat, but it didn't move. She sat there wondering what to do next.

"Can I help?" Ruth heard a voice behind her. She turned around and found Jacob looking down at the goat. Maybe he had heard her entreaties with the goat. She looked at him and he looked calmer than a few minutes ago.

Ruth nodded and Jacob sat down beside her. He took the goat in his hands and examined the wound. "It is a deep cut. How did this happen?"

"I am not sure. The goat is not one of ours. We found the goat and her kid at the foothills. Apparently, a branch had fallen over it. The goat is badly wounded and will not get up."

Jacob patted the goat and cooed silently to it. He rubbed its neck. The goat opened its eyes to look at the newcomer.

"Can you give me that pot of water?" Jacob asked.

Ruth handed over the pot of water and watched as Jacob gently cleaned the goat's wound. Ruth was astounded. The goat had squirmed a lot when she had cleaned its wounds yesterday. Now, it was sitting still in Jacob's lap.

Ruth said, "You do have a way with animals."

Jacob smiled quietly as he cleaned the wound. "I am fond of animals. Maybe they also get fond of me. Back home, I manage all the animals on our farm."

"That's wonderful to know."

Jacob nodded. "When I was a child, I climbed up a tree because I was afraid of my neighbor's dog. I was scared of the animals on my farm as well. My father helped me overcome my fear of animals and replace it with love. In fact, last week he ..." Jacob stopped, as a realization crushed his soul. His father was no longer in his life.

Ruth watched Jacob, understanding the turmoil going through his mind. She patted his shoulder. "Everything will be all right."

"No. Everything will not be all right." Jacob shouted.

Ruth was stunned at his response. She wasn't sure what to say. Feeling awkward, she looked down and arranged the folds of her skirt hoping that Mary would arrive and rescue her from Jacob's presence.

"I am sorry, Miss Byler." Jacob said after a moment. "I didn't mean to offend you. The last few days have been tough on me. I am not usually like this." Jacob sighed.

Ruth gave a noncommittal shrug.

Jacob pointed at the goat. It had closed its eyes and lay motionless. "The goat is very weak. I am not sure if it will survive, let alone ever stand again."

"No, that can't be!" Ruth was anguished.

Jacob kept quiet.

"I will pray to God to cure the goat. God will listen to me." Ruth said.

Jacob had a faraway look. "God didn't listen to me."

Ruth was perplexed. "Pardon me?"

Jacob turned to Ruth. "God didn't listen to my prayers when my father was sick. I saw my father wilting away under the strain of the disease. I prayed from my heart, but my father's condition worsened with each passing day. Eventually, he died. And I could do nothing to save him." Tears started to trickle from Jacob's eyes.

Ruth clutched Jacob's shoulder in compassion. She wasn't sure how to console him.

Jacob continued. "I was a faithful disciple of the Lord. I had prayed to Him every day of my life. I was a good follower of God. Alas, it came to naught. Why would He allow such a terrible thing to happen to His people?"

"I don't know. But I do know that good

deeds reap good results. We may not see the results we want today, but our unquestioning faith in the Lord will eventually be manifested in having a blessed life."

Jacob looked at Ruth with a pained expression. "But it's so hard. I can't bear the pain I am going through. I'm not sure I'm strong enough to bear this burden."

"You don't know how strong you are, until being strong is the only option you have."

Jacob dwelled on what Ruth said. With his father's loss, there was no one as the head of the family. His mother had done what she could. She sent them away so that the change of scenery could help them. He suddenly realized the great strength his mother displayed for making the choice to be alone during this time. *What about me? Am I facing my challenges with strength? Or with excuses?*

Ruth continued. "The Lord carried the cross with nary a word. We also have to carry our own crosses. The Lord told us to keep our faith in Him. And He said that those who keep faith in Him will be rewarded for their faith." Ruth looked at Jacob. "We may at times not understand His will, but we have to keep faith in Him and not lean on our understanding."

Jacob didn't answer. His mind was on the final days of his father's life. He remembered being heartbroken when he first heard the doctor say that his father had a few days to live. It had been too much for his young ears to hear. The scream that had followed was like a tormented soul in hell. Except for him, it was hell on earth. The hell had grown worse with each passing day culminating in the victory of Death. Mercifully, it had been a painless death with his father passing away in his sleep. Jacob remembered the last words his father had said to him. *God will show you the path.*

He thought about what Ruth said. *Am I resisting God's will? Is He showing me a path and I'm being blind to it?* He still couldn't understand why his father had passed away. But there was something in what Ruth had said. He remembered the Biblical quote that she had spoken from: *Trust in the Lord with all your heart and lean not on your own understanding; in all your ways submit to Him, and He will make your paths straight.*

* * * *

Mary came in. "I kept the kid in the second pen with the other goat."

Jacob was intrigued. "Why is that?"

Ruth explained. "She was pulling at her mother's bandages. We had to get the kid someplace far so that the goat's wounds have a chance to heal."

Jacob shook his head. "It doesn't look like the wound is healing quickly enough. It is also bleeding a little. We will need to stop the bleeding first."

"We can dab a little turmeric on the wound," said Ruth, remembering her days at the apothecary.

"That's an excellent suggestion."

Ruth went to the house and came back in a minute with a bowl of powdered turmeric. Jacob applied it to the wound. The bleeding minimized. He kept applying the turmeric till the bleeding stopped. Jacob tied a fresh cloth around the goat's leg.

Jacob said, "Let's monitor the goat's progress for the next two days."

"Thank you. You have been a great help to us today," Ruth expressed her gratitude.

Jacob nodded somberly. "Today is the first time in three days that I didn't think of my father every other minute. I should be the one to thank you."

"Jacob Miller?" a voice spoke behind them.

Jacob stood up and greeted the visitor. "Yes, Father Bontrager, how may I help?"

"The Bishop would like to speak with you," said the Bishop's advisor. "He will meet you tomorrow morning at his home."

Ruth saw Jacob pause on hearing Father Bontrager's words. Jacob finally said, "Yes, Father."

"Thank you." Father Bontrager left.

Ruth came to Jacob's side. "What would the Bishop want from you? You are not from here."

Jacob watched the receding figure. "Looks like I am in trouble."

"Why?"

"Father Bontrager was at my Uncle's home the other day. I expressed my unhappiness with God in his presence."

"What will happen now?"

"Let's talk with Uncle."

* * * *

Chapter 6

"You should have been more restrained in your words, son."

Jacob looked down on the wooden floor. He fiddled with his straw hat. He could feel his Uncle's gaze on him. His cheeks burned with

shame. *I have made things difficult for my Uncle.*
He knew that his Uncle was unhappy with him,
but his Uncle was not known to be outspoken.
He would simply point out the errors of Jacob's
ways.

Jacob looked up at Ruth and felt
embarrassed. He wished Ruth wasn't seeing him
in such a situation. He admired her simple
beauty and was afraid she would think worse of
him. He turned to his Uncle. His Uncle's eyes
were expectant, waiting for him to say
something.

Jacob's mind went back to the argument
he had with his Uncle. Jacob had been very
angry. The trauma of the past few days had
bubbled out like a volcano. He regretted the
words he had said. And Father Bontrager had
heard Jacob declare his loss of faith and his
anger against God for taking away his father.
And now, his Uncle could lose the respect of the

community if others learned of Jacob's outburst.

Jacob said, "I need to make amends for what I have done. I will meet the Bishop and apologize to him."

Mr. Miller said, "It is not as easy as you think. We don't know what Father Bontrager may have told him. Let me have a word with the Bishop."

"No. This is all my fault. I should be the one to apologize."

"Are you being adamant again, Jacob?" His Uncle asked in a firm tone.

Jacob sunk his head. He was making things worse for everyone. He realized he had been self-centered to the point of ignoring everyone.

Ruth interjected. "If I may say, I don't

think its Jacob's fault."

Jacob's ears perked up. He hadn't expected Ruth to say something on his behalf.

Mr. Miller spoke up. "I think I will be the judge of that."

Ruth continued. "Yes, Mr. Miller. But, he is going through a tough phase, and we should be supportive of him. If he wants to meet the Bishop, I think you should let him. If he has done wrong, he is right in asking to be the one to mend things. Let him face the Bishop, and take his due for his deeds."

Mr. Miller contemplated Ruth's words for a minute and then spoke. "Ruth, you do have a point. He should face the repercussions of his deeds." He turned to Jacob. "You can speak with the Bishop tomorrow, but a word of caution. Do not speak in haste. Measure your words and then speak."

"I will, Uncle."

"You do that, Jacob. I fear the situation doesn't bode well for you."

Ruth asked, "What do you think will happen, Mr. Miller?"

Mr. Miller sighed. "In the best case, he will be warned. In the worst case, he will be shunned."

* * * *

Chapter 7

Jacob waited outside the Bishop's door. He clutched the chair tightly, as if the physical contact would give him the necessary support. Cold sweat broke through his hairline. He had slept fitfully the previous night. A lot depended on this meeting. He consciously reminded himself to be restrained in his words.

"The Bishop will meet you now." Father Bontrager gave him a cold look. Jacob ignored him and went inside. The Bishop's room was spartan. After glancing around, he greeted the Bishop. The Bishop had been checking his correspondence based on the pile of letters in front of him. Jacob wondered what Father Bontrager had told the Bishop. He didn't have to wait long to find out.

"Son, Father Bontrager told me that yours is a case of lost faith."

Jacob paused for a moment and then said, "Yes Reverend, that is correct."

"Have you completed your *rumspringa*?"

"Yes, I have."

"That indicates that you made a commitment to be a church member and follow the path of God."

"Yes, that's correct."

"Well, why the change of heart?"

Jacob inhaled deeply. He wasn't sure where the conversation was going. The best resort was to explain everything sincerely and hope for the best. "My father died a few days ago. It has been hard for me to cope with the loss. I might have inadvertently said a few things that I shouldn't. I apologize for my mistake."

"Would I be correct in assuming that you were a faithful devotee before your father's death?"

"Yes, Reverend, I was. However, I would like to know why did God take away my father?

He was a good, honest person who had never done any evil."

The Bishop nodded, more at himself than at Jacob. "The Lord works in mysterious ways." He picked up one of the letters in front of him. "This is a letter from the Bishop of a neighboring community. One of the ladies there had lost her faith in God because she was getting old and no one had married her. Last week she got married, and her faith in God is now unshakeable. Why do you think that happened?"

Jacob kept quiet. He didn't know the answer.

The Bishop continued. "Faith is a living breathing thing. Faith cannot be static, because it stems from emotions. Your faith will change for better or worse over the course of a lifetime, based on how your life is going at that moment. And that is natural."

"But I don't think I can recover my faith after seeing what happened to my father," Jacob interjected.

The Bishop smiled. "I cannot force you to believe in His will. No one can. It's up to you to decide what you want to believe in. The choices you make will determine your life. And know this. *Faith is also a choice.* It is up to you to believe in it or not. When we believe in God, we learn to walk in faith and trust God. But first we must believe, and it's up to us. No one can teach you faith. It comes from within. It comes down to what you choose for your life... unshakeable faith or endless doubt."

Jacob said, "I don't have any doubts."

The Bishop was firm. "As I said, I cannot convince you to keep faith in God. I will be sending a note to the Bishop of your village informing him of our discussion. He will be better suited to take a decision in this matter."

Jacob sighed. The Bishop of his village would inform his mother. His mother would be embarrassed at Jacob's behavior.

Things were not looking good.

* * * *

Chapter 8

"What did the Bishop have to say?" Ruth was curious. She had seen Jacob returning back to his house and had hastened to his side.

Jacob looked at Ruth. "The Bishop will be reporting my behavior to my local Bishop. If my mother comes to know of it, and I am sure she will, she will cringe with shame. Alas, I have made things worse, not just for myself but for my Uncle and *Mudder* too."

Ruth grasped Jacob's arm. "Don't despair.

We will think of something. There is always a way out."

"Ruth!" she heard Mary hailing her from the farm. "You have to come look at the goat!"

Ruth was intrigued. She had forgotten about the goat. Her mind had been on Jacob's situation. The bleeding had stopped yesterday and Ruth had been mildly optimistic of the goat being restored back to health. She hurried over to Mary, with Jacob behind her.

"What happened?" Ruth asked.

Mary led them to the pen. The goat was lying on the ground motionless.

"Is … is it dead?" Ruth held her breath.

"No, but it refuses to eat anything."

"Oh, what are we to do?" Ruth was worried.

Jacob stepped in. "Let me have a look."

Jacob took the goat in his arms and examined it. He removed the cloth around its legs and examined the wound. The wound had clotted which was a good sign. He rubbed the goat's body and massaged its head. The goat opened its eyes and bleated weakly. He offered a clump of grass but the goat wouldn't eat it.

Jacob looked up at Ruth. "I am sorry. The goat is very weak. It may not survive."

Ruth started crying. Jacob was sorry. He held her shoulders and tried to console her. Ruth looked at Jacob with tear-filled eyes. "I had so much wanted to save the goat."

A terrible sense of *déjà vu* crept over Jacob. He had seen his father pass away. He had felt helpless. Now, the goat was in his arms and he again felt helpless.

The tears started rolling down his eyes.

* * * *

"Jacob, I've been looking everywhere for you. You ..." Mr. Miller stopped short as he saw both Ruth and Jacob crying. "What's the matter? Is everything all right?"

Ruth wiped her eyes. "The goat is about to die."

Mr. Miller was no stranger to death of farm animals. "Oh! That's a pity. But are we sure there's nothing we can do about it?"

"I don't know." Ruth said in between sobs.

Jacob said in a monotone. "I was not able to save my father, and now I am unable to save this goat. I am the one to blame."

Mr. Miller was surprised. "Now Jacob, you are being foolish. Your father died due to a terminal illness."

"No, he died because I didn't do anything to save him. If I had more faith, I could have saved his life."

Mr. Miller wrapped his arm around Jacob. "Sometimes, everything that you do may not turn out to be enough. When I was of your age, I had married your Aunt Martha and we were expecting our first child. Your Aunt went into labor and delivered the baby. But the baby didn't cry or move. It was stillborn. I pleaded with the doctors to revive it. They did try. I prayed to God for our child. But the baby didn't survive. Your Aunt Martha was distraught, and felt guilty over the loss of the child. But was it really her fault? Would pining away in guilt bring back the child? Jacob, if you were in my place, what would you have told her?"

Jacob looked down at the goat in his

arms. He wondered if he was acting in the same way as his Aunt had done. Living a life of guilt. *Am I being too harsh on myself?* Jacob finally spoke. "I would have told her to move on. Being guilty was serving no purpose. Acceptance of the loss, and moving on was more important at the moment than dwelling on the past."

Mr. Miller said, "Exactly. That is precisely what I told her. Now would you think this advice applies to you?"

"I suppose it does."

Mr. Miller was happy to see that Jacob was seeing the light. "Our past cannot be changed. But we can change what we do today. We can choose to be in the present and change our future. Being guilty will not help you or others. You have to look past the guilt and ask what you can do to overcome it. And once you do, you will be able to see the path that God has laid for you."

* * * *

Ruth had also listened closely to Mr. Miller's story. The scales fell off her eyes as she realized that she had felt guilty at her association with the *Englischer*. Her father hadn't said anything to her. It was time she also moved on and stopped feeling guilty about her past. Her today mattered more. She couldn't let the guilt from her past hold her future hostage. Ruth felt a calmness all over her.

Jacob breathed deeply. "I also need to let go of my guilt. It is not helping anyone, especially myself. I always wanted my father to be proud of me. He was always devoted to God. I will carry on that path."

Mr. Miller nodded. "That's true, son. Take refuge in the power of prayer. If you have faith, you can move mountains."

Sandra Becker

* * * *

Chapter 9

Jacob prayed fervently to God. It had been a few days since he had last prayed, but never before had he poured so much faith in his prayer to God. He now knew that the goat was going to be saved, and he only had to ask God for His blessings.

Jacob finished his prayers. He looked at Ruth and could see her lips moving in silent prayer. He was grateful to Ruth for her support in the past few days. She had even supported him in front of his Uncle. He wondered what made her support him. He couldn't find a reason. Maybe it was God's will. He promised himself that he would do whatever he could to keep Ruth happy.

Jacob went over to the pen to check on the goat. The goat's condition hadn't improved. It blinked its eyes blankly at him.

Ruth arrived at his side. "It's still not eating the grass. If it doesn't eat, it will die."

Jacob said, "I don't think we have done enough."

Ruth said, "We have prayed a lot for the poor creature."

"There is faith, and there is works."

"What do you suggest?"

Jacob said, "I just remembered something I saw on my own farm. You separated the calf from its mother."

Ruth said, "Yes, the kid had aggravated the mother's wound."

"I think the kid could save the mother."

Ruth was surprised. "How is that

possible? The kid is the reason the mother is in such a weak state."

"Yes, but the power of love is greater than the power of death."

"What do you want me to do?"

Jacob smiled. "The mother needs to have a will to live. Bring over the kid."

Ruth went to the other pen and brought the kid. As soon as it saw its mother, the kid started licking her face and eyes. The mother goat opened her eyes wider and responded. She also licked the kid.

Ruth was thrilled. "Maybe it's working! Help her up."

Jacob lifted the mother goat on its legs. He egged the goat to move towards the kid. The little kid jumped around playfully urging its mother to do the same.

The mother opened its eyes wide, and walked haltingly towards the kid. It nuzzled its face to the kid's body. Jacob offered some grass to the goat and it took the blades gingerly.

Ruth was amazed. "You are right. She now has a will, a reason to live."

As Jacob watched the mother goat eating the grass, he realized that all was well. He should have put more faith in the Lord. But Jacob knew that it was better late than never.

Jacob closed his eyes and started praying. He asked for God's forgiveness for doubting His will. And he made a commitment that he would follow God's path, no matter where He would lead. Jacob breathed deeply.

He was finally at peace with himself.

* * * *

Ruth was happy. The goat looked in much better shape after eating the grass. Jacob had used his experience to save the goat's life. She was eternally grateful to him for what he had done. Ruth looked at Jacob and found him in prayer. She smiled. Jacob had rediscovered his faith. She heard a voice close behind.

"Jacob Miller! I see that your faith triumphed in the end."

She turned and saw Father Bontrager. The Father was all smiles to see Jacob pray. Jacob replied. "Yes, Father. Faith triumphs all obstacles."

Father Bontrager said, "I am happy to see that you are on the right path. I will inform the Bishop that you have reformed your ways."

Ruth looked at Jacob and smiled. She was happy at how things had come nicely together.

Maybe, God has a plan for everyone.

* * End Of Part II* *

3. GOD WILL SHOW THE PATH

Chapter 1

Jacob had invaded her thoughts.

It was past midnight and Ruth couldn't sleep. Instead, she was thinking of all the time they'd so far spent together, and how much she still felt like it was not enough. Ruth believed deep down in her heart that *Gott* had sent Jacob to be her husband. Her love for him continued to grow every day... every hour... every minute.

But, when would he ask?

****

She woke with the sunrise. Even after losing a few hours of sleep to her thoughts Ruth felt ready to take on the day. Just like she had every morning for as long as she could remember, she closed her eyes and surrendered herself to God. With her eyes closed, she could focus clearly and Ruth prayed and gave heartfelt thanks for the loving family and life God had granted her. She could hear the crowing of the rooster out on the farm and the chirping of the birds from a nearby tree. A small smile crept up her face.

God has given me another wonderful day to follow His path.

After her prayers, she focused on her daily duties. It was always the same... washing and hanging the laundry out to dry in the sun when it was warm, cleaning the dishes, and tending to the animals in the barn.

If she was lucky, she'd run into Jacob. Her stomach did a back flip at the thought. Jacob had moved to their town two weeks ago, and had helped her family the last few days. After helping her save one of the kids on her family's farm, her father had become convinced that he needed the boy as his right hand. Ruth suspected that her parents wanted him as close as possible to see for themselves if he'd make a good husband for her. Even then, she was not certain they were destined to spend the rest of their lives together, and she wouldn't be sure until he asked.

Ruth went over to the wooden closet and changed into an old house dress, one of the ones her mother didn't like. She'd loved it years ago when Ruth had sewn it herself with scraps of fabric she'd found laying around the house but now that she wore it absolutely everywhere, even as it was falling apart, the only thing her mother hadn't done was throw it out herself. Considering that her mother never wanted to throw anything away, it meant that the dress really did need doing away with.

Ruth walked into the kitchen expecting an earful and found her mother bustling around while her younger sister Mary sat at the small table in the middle of the room kneading bread.

"*Gut* morning *schweschder*," Mary called, looking up for a brief moment before turning her attention back to the task at hand.

"We're making bread to send down to the market with your father when he goes this afternoon," her mother Emma said.

"Oh, yes. I heard Father mentioning it yesterday." Ruth sat down at the table next to her sister. Mary kept kneading the dough poking it in between to make sure it was soft and perfect for the customers.

Ruth fought the temptation to pluck a

piece of dough from the mound in her sister's hands and stick it into her mouth.

"Ruth, please don't eat the raw dough, it's really bad for you," her mother said as though she was reading her mind.

Ruth laughed. "I haven't even –"

"And..." her mother added. "If you keep dressing like that you're never going to get married! You sew beautifully. Why don't you make a new dress for church service? People who don't use their *Gott* given talents may one day lose them."

"Okay *mudder*," Ruth shook her head. "I don't see anything wrong with this dress that a few patches won't fix, but I will do away with it as you say. I will make another dress, but because I want to, and not because I am worried about marriage."

Her mother smiled and turned away. *"Wunderbaar.* Jacob's out in the field. He's already called for you this morning."

Without thinking about it, her back stiffened, and Ruth found herself at a loss for words. Jacob had already called for her? He usually waited for her out in the barn.

Perhaps today's the day he'd ask...

A surge on anticipation filled her heart. "Maybe I will change my dress," Ruth said.

"I have an old one you can wear," her mother said, washing her hands and scurrying off to her room. Ruth followed her through the living room where her father was fast asleep on the rug in front of the fireplace. She knew he'd been up all night chopping wood and getting his buggy ready for his trip to the market.

"Here is it," her mother called as she

walked into the small room her parents shared.

Her mother held up a thick black dress that looked nearly identical to the one she was now wearing, other than the fact that it was much less worn.

"There's a nice hidden pocket in the front that you can use to store things," she said. "I know you're always carrying bits and pieces to and fro' from the farm."

"*Mudder*, it's nice," Ruth said. "I will wear it."

She turned away feeling the heat creep up to her cheeks.

"Go on," her mother encouraged. "Put it on."

Ruth turned away glad for the dimly lit room that hid her flushed cheeks and the embarrassment of trying to look nice for a boy. She and her mother wrestled the first dress off her body, and then she slipped into the new one.

"You look as beautiful as always," her mother said with a smile. "It doesn't matter so much what you wear but it's nice to have a new dress sometimes. Your *ant* Martha made this one for me, now it is yours to keep."

Ruth hugged her mother and they both made their way back to the kitchen. By then, her father Samuel was awake and had joined them next to the fireplace. Ruth peered into the kitchen and saw that Mary was still working her fingers into the dough like her life depended on it.

"Samuel," Ruth's mother said walking towards her father. "Jacob's here."

"*Ach*," said her father.

"We should meet his *mudder* soon," her mother said gesturing to Ruth.

Her father nodded. "Jacob is a nice boy, and you like him, Ruth?"

Ruth's cheeks were flaming hot again. She didn't want to have this conversation with her parents.

"Yes, she likes him," her mother said smiling, and patting her on the shoulder. "They are happy in each others' company. We will talk to his *mudder* soon."

Pulling her cloak over her dress Ruth hastily backed out of the room. Her parents continued talking and she grabbed her boots and slipped out the back door. Surely nature would distract her from their words and the thoughts that had stolen her sleep.

*****

Ruth always looked forward to summers in Lancaster County and the sunshine beaming down on that beautiful June morning filled her with hope. Everything would be just fine, and even Jacob would ask her soon enough. She wondered if that was why he'd come calling so early, and ran across the field to find him. She spotted Jacob cleaning out the barn and walked over to him unnoticed. She came around the corner of the barn taking him by surprise.

Jacob stumbled backward and let out a shout of surprise.

"You startled me," he said.

"Sorry," Ruth smiled, looking down at the grass. Her heart was pounding wildly. "You're up early today."

"Yes, there is something I wanted to tell

you." Jacob said.

Okay, here it comes. Ruth fidgeted with the folds of her dress. But Jacob didn't speak. She wondered if he was nervous. Ruth turned to look at him and found that Jacob seemed distracted. He looked at the morning sun peeking out from behind the hills, then back at her. There was a sadness in his eyes she hadn't seen before.

"I don't have much time. I'm going back home today and the trip takes about two hours."

"You're going home?" she asked in surprise. "Why?"

He paused and dug his pitch fork into the ground.

"I need to be with my family," Jacob twisted the pitch fork deeper in the wet soil.

Ruth noticed that he was still not looking at her. She wondered why he'd taken so long to tell her.

"It'll be alright," he said gruffly.

"Why didn't you let me know sooner?"

He shook his head.

"How is your *mudder*?" Ruth asked.

"Not good..."

She waited for him to say more but he just stood there.

"I'll be gone for a little while," he said finally.

Her heart was breaking at his sadness. She knew that Jacob had been having a hard time coping with his father's death but she hadn't expected to hear that he was leaving.

"I'm really sorry about your father Jacob..."

"It was *Gott*'s will. Now he can rest."

Jacob's voice was breaking. Ruth felt torn between her disappointment that he didn't propose to her, and the realization that Jacob really needed to be with his mother. But he was right. His place was by his mother's side.

Ruth took a deep breath to compose herself, and asked forgiveness from the Lord for her self-centered intentions. "*Mudder* is doing some baking; you'll take some bread with you for the journey?"

"That would be nice..." he said, his sparkly blue eyes finally settling on her face. "You'll be alright?"

Jacob was the one who'd lost a parent, yet he was concerned about her.

"I will miss you." Ruth said.

"I'll be back..."

"When?"

Jacob hesitated. "I don't know..."

They lingered in silence for a moment, then he grabbed her hand into his own. She was so startled that she almost jumped back and pulled her hand away. Something in his eyes convinced her to stay. He looked at her, then turned around wordlessly and walked away. She watched him disappear into the trees, not sure when she'd see him again.

Chapter 2

Jacob closed his eyes in anguish. *If only I could tell her how supportive her presence had been in the last few days.*

Walking away from Ruth was one of the hardest things he'd ever had to do. Jacob wished he'd had the strength to let her family know that he was leaving. If he knew Ruth's father well, he'd have tried to convince him to stay. Or, he'd have offered to drive Jacob and his brother Isaac back home in his buggy. Jacob wanted to do things on his own. The two hour journey would at least give him some time to clear his head before returning home.

The last two days had been a blur. He'd gotten a letter from his mother telling him that things were not going well with the farm. Though he and his younger brother Isaac helped out when they could, their father had been the primary breadwinner for the family. With his passing, some of that responsibility now belonged to the boys.

Ruth's father had paid Jacob for the last week of work and Jacob felt satisfied that he had made a modest amount that would help them somewhat back home. As the elder of the two siblings Jacob felt as though it was his responsibility to ensure they had enough food on the table for their family. He was now expected to be the breadwinner of the family.

Walking from Ruth's family's farm to Uncle Miller's took a few minutes. Jacob hadn't brought the buggy over to work that day as he'd feared it would raise suspicions to arrive with it already packed when he hadn't even told Ruth or her family that he was leaving. Waiting to share his news hadn't done him any good. This was something people needed to be prepared for. Even so, preparation hadn't seemed a consideration for his father's departure.

Jacob arrived home to the smell of freshly baked bread and immediately remembered Ruth's thoughtful offer and felt ashamed for having left so abruptly.

"Jacob?" *ant* Martha called from the kitchen window.

"Yes *ant*."

"I've packed you and Isaac some bread for the trip. I made some meat, vegetables and cooked up some stew. That should last you a couple of days so your mother won't have to do much cooking. Poor dear. I've been praying for her every night all alone on that farm. I'm so glad you boys are going home to be with her."

"Yes *ant*, me too."

Isaac appeared from another room and took the two large packages from Aunt Martha.

"Go ahead and put them into the buggy," Jacob instructed.

Isaac nodded and walked out the door.

"All set?"

"Just about. Where's uncle?"

"He's out front fixing the wheels on your buggy. You might have passed him by."

Jacob went outside and saw his uncle sitting next to the well. He was wiping the sweat off his face with a cloth.

"Best you boys get along before noon," Uncle Miller said. "I've tightened the bolts on the wheels, so you won't have any trouble."

Jacob watched as the older man slowly

got to his feet. Uncle Miller was a jack of all trades. He knew how to do everything, from fixings buggies, to farming, and he'd even worked as a carpenter for a while like their father.

"Well son," he said. "I pray you have a safe journey. Keep asking *Gott* to show you the way. He's there for you even in the toughest times."

"Thank you uncle," Jacob said. "I really appreciate all you've done."

Isaac hopped into the buggy with a quiet prayer. He had sought refuge in the Lord to help him grieve for his father's death.

"Take care of your brother and give your mom our regards," said Aunt Martha, who'd joined them in the front yard.

"I will. I'll be back as soon as I can."

"Don't worry son, I'll talk to the Bylers' for you. They'll understand."

Jacob nodded and hopped into the buggy. Their aunt and uncle waved as they pulled away from the house that had been their home for the last two weeks.

Jacob and Isaac rode along in silence, Jacob's mind flooded with memories of things he hadn't thought about in a while. Shortly after his father Eli had passed away her mother had arranged for Jacob and Isaac to move in with Uncle Miller and Aunt Martha. She'd thought a change of scenery would do them good, so the brothers moved in with Uncle Miller and his wife whose children had already moved on to start their own families.

The Byler family lived next door to Uncle Miller's farm and Jacob had met Ruth for the first time when he and his brother had been invited to their house for *Fastnacht*. They hadn't spoken much that night, but sometime after that he'd helped her nurse one of the kids on her family's farm back to health after it had caught pneumonia from being accidentally left out in the cold. That one instance had built both of their faith and they'd been drawn to each other from that day. After that he'd started helping out on the farm more and more, until he worked there nearly every day.

He and Isaac grew close to the Byler family in the short time they were there. Everyone in the neighborhood knew them as Uncle Miller's boys, even though he wasn't their father. Now that their mother needed them, Jacob felt that he had no choice but to put his family before any prospect of a future with Ruth.

"I feel like I've abandoned *mudder*," Jacob

said as they bumped along down the rugged road.

"Don't feel that way... *mudder* thought it was best we were given some time to get over father's passing away."

"I feel like things would have been different if we'd never left."

Isaac stared out into the surrounding forest. "I don't know," he said. "What could we have done?"

He was right. The last couple months of their father's life had been stressful for all of them, but none more so than for their mother who'd been taking care of him. Jacob hoped returning home now would make up for their absence. The sun was at its peak and they were leaving the good old village behind to return to the home where they had been raised.

****

"Well does he love you or not?"

Sarah was propped up in a small space next to the kitchen sink listening to Ruth as she cleaned the dishes. Ruth had told Sarah about the events of the morning. An hour ago, Aunt Miller had informed her mother that the brothers had left. She had overheard their conversation in silence, determined not to be angry at Jacob for his unannounced exit. But as much as she tried to rationalize Jacob's actions under the influence of his father's death, disappointment crept up into her thoughts. It didn't help that Sarah also felt the same way on learning about Jacob's behavior.

"I don't know for sure. I think he does, but so far he hasn't proposed or given any clear indication."

"Hmm. What if he thinks about you as

just a friend, and nothing more?"

Ruth stopped washing the dishes midway. "You mean he is not interested in me?" she looked up at Sarah.

"It could be possible."

Ruth twirled the dish absent-mindedly in her hand; Sarah's suggestion taking root in her mind. She shook her head. "No. I've seen it in his eyes. I know he's the one for me." Ruth said out loud, more to convince herself than Sarah.

"Well, if that's the case why didn't he say something before he left?" Sarah countered.

Ruth reflected on the question. It wasn't a question she'd dare ask herself. But it couldn't be ignored. Jacob had left. And she didn't know when he would be back.

Or if he would want to.

Chapter 3

Miriam watched as the old kerosene lamp burnt dimly in the distance. The house was quiet now that Eli wasn't around. Things had been pretty dismal ever since Eli had fallen sick, but had deteriorated even more once he'd passed away. He'd fainted and fallen sick one day out on the farm, and Miriam had called for his brother Miller right away. When Miller and Martha finally arrived they'd all prayed together and Eli had seemed to be in better spirits. By chance, an *Englischer* nurse had been in town that week and she'd come over with a neighbor to see Eli. It was she who had confirmed Eli's condition, and had revealed that it would be a matter of a few months. The last few weeks of Eli's life had been spent managing his ailing condition, and even in the worst of times Eli had been comforted by the fact that *Gott* would take care of him.

"Whatever happens, Miriam," he'd said a few days before he'd passed. "It is *Gott*'s will."

Running her fingers over an unfinished knit blanket, Miriam pressed her back into the wooden couch she and her late husband had spent many evenings sitting in and praying together. She believed what had happened was *Gott*'s will, and that there was nothing anyone could have done to change it. Not even her. Still, sitting alone at the fireplace in an empty house brought tears to her eyes.

It had been a little over two weeks since her husband her died. The grief had ebbed leaving behind a dull ache. The void of her husband's absence though was felt every moment. Whether, it was waking with the first light and turning in her bed to see if her husband had got up before her; and then realizing that he wasn't there for her. At dinner time, she would pull out her husband's favorite plate and then ruefully putting it back, knowing that he would no longer be at the table to share the meals. She would wait in the evening for the inevitable knock that signaled her husband coming home after a day's work at the farm, but the knock never came about.

Why did God leave her all alone to face it?

Jacob and Isaac would be home soon... then she wouldn't be alone. Then she'd have help, and some more time to finish her knitting. Perhaps the boys would be able to mind the farm and the wood shop, just like their father had. It was too much of a sad time to think about the bills that would soon start piling up if someone didn't take up breadwinner duties, but continuing on even in times of sadness was just the way life was.

Miriam raised her eyes skyward and offered a prayer to *Gott*. She prayed for Jacob and Isaac to be safe on their journey, and for peace upon herself and her household to cope with their unimaginable loss.

*****

Isaac turned his eyes from the rolling hills that could be seen from the buggy windows to his brother sitting next to him. Jacob was brooding all alone in his own thoughts.

The two hour ride felt like an eternity. For the entire trip home they sat in silence as the realization of the new direction their lives were about to take sunk in. Their father was no longer there to guide them now, and they were the men of the house. They would be responsible for the family now.

It meant making your own decisions. Decisions on how they would sustain their livelihood, and of course who they would marry, now that they were of suitable age.

Without his older brother having to say anything Isaac knew Jacob's heart was breaking at the thought of leaving Ruth. Jacob always put up a tough front but inside he was the most kindhearted and loving person Isaac knew. Only something like this would have led to him walking away from the love of his life. Isaac on the other hand had nothing to lose. He hadn't yet found a girl who liked him, or wanted to spend time with him. He didn't know the first thing about courting a young woman and had been hoping Jacob would be the one to get married first to show him the ropes. Now that would have to wait.

*****

Jacob pulled the buggy to an abrupt stop just before turning into the lane leading to their home. The afternoon sun was low in the sky, but he could see the house clearly, the small cottage in the midst of a wide, expansive barn. Other than time period of two weeks, nothing had changed. He was the same person returning to the same place. The only thing different now was that he would walk into the house and his father Eli would be nowhere to be found. He felt Isaac's questioning eyes burning into his skin but Jacob didn't make any attempt to move the buggy.

"You alright?" Isaac asked. He might as well not have spoken. Jacob's mind was so far away that they might as well have been in separate places.

"It's going to be okay *bruder*," Isaac said, following Jacob's gaze to the field of grazing animals. "*Mudder* will be happy to see us both. Now she will have company, and not just the animals."

Jacob looked at his brother and nodded somberly.

*****

Two solemn knocks were all it took to send Miriam rushing for the door. She opened the door to the faces of her beloved sons, Jacob and Isaac, both looking like spitting images of their father. Immediately, she broke down into tears and felt her strength leave her body. Jacob reached out to catch her before she fell, and he and Isaac guided her back to the chair.

"*Ach*," Isaac said sitting down next to Miriam. "It's good to see you. Please, don't fret. *Gott* is good, he will help us."

"I know child," Miriam sobbed. "Eli was such a good man."

"*Mudder*," Jacob said reaching over to touch Miriam's shoulder. "I am so sorry."

Miriam looked at Jacob. "What for?"

"For leaving you all alone."

"It's okay, my child."

"No mother. When you sent me, I was too consumed in my grief, to realize your sacrifice. I will never leave you again."

Miriam wiped her eyes and looked at her sons. "I am happy you are back. I really missed you children. Please don't leave me alone."

Jacob's simmering guilt peaked. He felt anguished that it had taken him two weeks to see the situation from his mother's viewpoint. "What can we do?"

"I don't want to burden you," she said. "You have your own lives too."

"*Mudder*," Jacob said again more urgently this time. "What can we do? We want to help."

Miriam sighed. "There's the wood shop… and the farm that need tending to," she said finally. "With all my crochet work there's barely any time left over to mind the shop."

"Mother," Isaac said. "You know we'll do anything to help. This is our home."

"How bad is the situation?" Jacob asked gravely.

"Eli worked in the shop for many years, and out in the field. With him gone, we need someone to look after the shop and farm."

Jacob grunted, as though in pain, and looked away.

"But there is hope," Miriam said. "It will take some work but if we can get things going with the wood shop we'll be back on track."

The crackling fireplace was the only

sound to be heard. Miriam knew Jacob didn't like associating with the *Englischers* who frequented the wood shop. He was so much of an introvert that even his family sometimes wondered how he got himself to speak with them.

"Jacob, you helped Eli in the shop at times..." Miriam said. "Perhaps you can do that while Isaac tends to the fields."

Jacob nodded. He knew his mother was counting on him and Isaac.

"We came back to help," Isaac said. "And that's what we'll do."

"I am happy to have you back," Miriam said, feeling more at peace in the presence of her sons than she had in days. "We will pray to *Gott*. He will deliver us."

Chapter 4

Bright and early every day for the entire next week Jacob and Isaac worked the farm and minded the wood shop. One morning even before his mother was up and about; Jacob made his way to see the shop. He ran into Isaac on the way there.

"*Gut* morning *bruder,*" Isaac called cheerily. "I'm on my way to milk the cows. Then I'll sweep the cobwebs out of the barn and get some dust out. It's musty there."

"I'll bet," Jacob said, looking over his brother's shoulder at the barn that was in dire need of repair. "The roof looks like it could use a bit of nailing as well."

Isaac nodded. "I'll get to that a bit later in the week. For now it's the animals that need some care. The neighbor looked after them before we came, but I'll bet he has enough on his account already with that large plot of land of his own to look after."

"I'm about to go open up the shop," Jacob said. "I have to finish this armchair I'm working on.

Isaac smiled. "So that means you're getting on with it?"

Jacob shrugged. "I'm doing the best I can."

"That's all we can do," Isaac said. "What about Ruth? Did you reply to her letters yet?"

Jacob sighed. Ruth had written him nearly every day since he'd been gone but Jacob hadn't found any time to write back to her. Even in his free time he'd managed to come up with excuses. What good would it be for him to write her back when he didn't even know if they had a future together?

"I will when I'm not running around like a crazy chicken," Jacob joked.

"You sure?" Isaac asked.

"I will," Jacob assured him, still not sure when he'd find the time. "See you later."

*****

At least keeping busy had so far managed to take his mind off things. He was no woodwork master like his father but Jacob knew a thing or two about furniture making. He'd made up his mind to finish the armchair he'd started working on earlier in the week but things were not going so well. He'd been trying all morning to cut a stubborn piece of wood to the right proportions to make the last leg for the piece of furniture.

Jacob tried to concentrate on the scraper

and made gentle passes over the wood. His father had once told him that the polishing stage determined the skill of the carpenter. His father would start with a scraper, then use a handplane and finally use sandpaper to polish it.

Jacob tried to follow his father's instructions as best as he could remember, but he had been an apprentice. He never had done a complete woodwork by himself. He simply used to follow along whatever commands his father gave him, mostly involved with cutting. The finer polishing had always been his father's domain. He wondered when he would get comfortable with woodworking, so that he could spend less time in the workshop and get some time to reply back to Ruth.

Ruth! Just the thought of her brought feelings of exhilaration mixed with regret. He still wondered if he had been hasty that day to leave her in the manner that he had. Was he right to abandon her when he could clearly see the unmistakable love in her eyes?

He kept scraping the wood. No, it had been the right thing to do. It wouldn't be good to raise her hopes when he himself wasn't sure about the path his life was taking. His father's death had completely uprooted his life and shaken his faith. But Ruth had given him hope. A hope that redemption was possible and the future could be better than what it was today.

He measured the wood he had just scraped and groaned loudly. He had scraped the piece a quarter of an inch too much.

Jacob sighed. Carpentry was tedious work. Now he'd have to start all over again. Chucking the useless piece of wood into a corner of the room he picked up another piece that would now take him the best part of an hour to get into shape. He wondered how his father had done this for so long. One or two pieces of furniture were all he seemed capable of completing without getting frustrated. Was this really what *Gott* intended for him? To spend the rest of his life doing something he did not love? Jacob would have chosen being out in the field with the animals any day over this.

Just then he heard the sound of a buggy approaching. He peered out the window to find one of the shop's regular customers, an *Englischer*, making his way inside. Jacob hadn't seen the man since he'd moved back home, but he recognized him from back when he used to buy goods from his father. Mr. Wofford was his name, and he always came around to order antiques to sell in town.

"Jacob, my boy," the man greeted gruffly with a wrinkled smile. "How are you, son? Long time no see."

"Mr. Wofford," Jacob smiled. "It's good to see you too."

"How's is your father?" the older gentleman glanced around the place. "I don't see him today."

"I am sorry to inform you Mr. Wofford, but he passed away a couple of weeks ago."

Mr. Wofford's eyes widened. "I am so sorry to hear that. May his soul rest in peace." He patted Jacob's shoulder. "How are you coping? How is your mother?"

"It's hard, but we're getting there," Jacob said.

"It's a tremendous loss. But God's will be done. He has gone off to a fine place. You can be sure of that. Eli was a nice person."

Jacob smiled. At least his father had left a

good and lasting impression on all who'd been fortunate to know him.

"So you've taken over?"

"I have… Can I help you with anything?"

"I'm sure you can! What have you got?"

"Give me a moment," Jacob said as he headed to the back room to fetch some of the last pieces of work made by his father, and some newer pieces he'd managed to complete. When he got back to the front of the shop Mr. Wofford was busy picking up and examining the different pieces.

"I'll never be anything like him," Jacob confessed. "He was the best. No other like Eli."

"Nonsense," the older man said. "You're Amish. Carpentry runs in your blood. You're bound to excel at it if you really try. What have you got there?"

Jacob handed the pieces over to Mr. Wofford and watched as the man gave them the once over, and nodded his head in approval.

"See... what did I tell you? I can't even tell which ones you made from the ones Eli put together!"

Jacob smiled. He knew Mr. Wofford was just being polite.

"I'll take them."

They exchanged money, and Jacob helped the older man haul his purchases to his buggy.

"Do you like this work?" Mr. Wofford asked just as they finished loading the last piece into the buggy.

"It's a good way to pass the time," Jacob answered.

"But you don't love it?"

Jacob lifted his head and looked across at the now setting sun and shook his head.

"I love working with animals," he said. "That's something I can do all day long. I love breeding and taking care of horses."

"Well son, that's exactly what you should be doing. Life is short."

Jacob sighed and Mr. Wofford patted him on the back. "I know you're going to be just fine Jacob. You're a good man, just like your father was."

"Thank you Mr. Wofford. Best of luck with those pieces."

"Oh they'll be gone as soon as they hit the market." the older man laughed as he mounted onto the buggy. "Take care, son!"

Jacob stepped back and waved as he drove away. Mr. Wofford was nice for an *Englischer*. If only life were as simple as just doing what you loved.

*****

What's with this boy? Why doesn't he reply back?

It was late afternoon and Ruth sat down to write a letter to Jacob, but the words were not forthcoming. She shared at the blank page with incredulity. What was she doing? She had poured over all her thoughts and feelings in half dozen letters in the past two weeks. There was nothing more she could write about. She needed answers. To be precise, she wanted a reply from Jacob. She couldn't decide if she was angry or worried.

Ruth got up and went to the living room where her mother was stitching a patch over one of the clothes. "*Mudder*," she said. "I still haven't heard from Jacob."

"Give him some time dear," her mother said. "Have some faith. If you really want to know how he's doing you can go over and speak to his uncle next door."

Determined to find out what was going on Ruth pulled on her overalls and shoes and marched over to Jacob's uncle's farm. There she found Uncle Miller out in the field tending to one of his horses.

"Good afternoon, Mr. Miller!" she greeted.

"Hello Ruth," Uncle Miller said smiling widely. "Good to see you. How are you doing?"

"Not so well. I haven't heard from Jacob. I've written him a few times and well... I'm a little worried."

"*Ach...*" Uncle Miller said scratching his head. "Jacob might be busy taking up his father's duties. They've got a lot going on at the moment."

Ruth sighed. "Alright. I was just a little worried. Hopefully I'll hear from him soon. You have a good day!"

Waving to Jacob's uncle she skipped back to her house. But the concern in her heart didn't ease. Sure Jacob was busy, but how much time would it really take for him to let her know he was alright?

Chapter 5

Miriam let out a deep sigh. It was nice to have Jacob and Isaac back. Jacob was her first son and every time she looked at him she saw his father. His presence healed her heart and broke it at the same time. He and Isaac were doing all they could to help and she was grateful. Still, their efforts didn't seem to be enough. She'd seen how much work Jacob especially had been putting into the wood shop yet sales had more than halved.

A new Amish antiques store nearby that had been set up by *Englischers* was stealing away their most loyal customers. Creditors were now after the family and though Miriam had tried to keep it a secret from the boys they'd found out and were now more stressed than ever. Miriam wished she could go back to the days when life was simple.

*****

Ruth was tired of waiting for Jacob. She still hadn't heard from him, and his uncle hadn't been able to tell her anything else but that he was busy. That wasn't good enough for her. This was the man she wanted to marry. What if he was lying sick somewhere? Her friend Sarah had stopped by that morning on her way to the market with her eldest brother John, and Ruth had convinced her mother to let her go along with them to see Jacob. The market wasn't very far from where he lived, and John sensing her distress had even offered to drop her off there before heading to the market. She sat fuming for most of the trip, although Sarah tried as hard as she could to make her laugh. When they dropped her off, she marched off in a huff to Jacob's front door barely hearing Sarah's promises to return for her on their way back home from the market.

Ruth had a feeling she'd find him in the wood shop so she headed there first. She opened the door and barged in to a startled Jacob. Her anger melted at the sight of him. His piercing blue eyes looked right at her, and she forgot all the things she wanted to say. Ruth stood in the entryway and said nothing.

"Ruth?" he said walking over to her. "What are you doing here? How did you get here? It's so good to see you..."

She felt the need to pull him close, and her face turned crimson at the thought. She had no right thinking those kinds of thoughts about a man who had yet to ask her to marry him.

"I wrote you so many letters," Ruth said quietly.

"I know," Jacob said thinking about the way he'd meant to respond that evening. "I haven't had any time to..."

"You had no time to write me just once," she said shakily. "You don't care for me, do you?"

"Of course I care about you," Jacob said dejectedly. "Don't you care for me? I've been busy doing my father's work."

"I understand that," she said. "But you didn't even come to see me once, and look how easy it was for me to get here. I need more from you Jacob!"

*****

Jacob knew she was right. He didn't want to argue with Ruth. Not with her standing there looking like a vision of radiance, even in her frustration.

"When will we see each other again?" Ruth asked.

"I don't know," Jacob felt helpless.

"Then I don't know either," she said as a tear slipped down her face. With a long and lingering look she turned around on her heel and stomped out of the shop.

"Ruth!" Jacob shouted running out after her. By the time he got to the door Ruth had already taken off in a sprint towards the market. There would be no following her now, and even if he did, what would he say? He didn't have any of the answers to the questions she was asking. He wanted to be with her as much as she did, but he didn't even know whether he was coming or going lately.

Jacob walked back into the shop thinking about the way Ruth had surprised him and come in like a whiff of fresh air. He'd forgotten how wonderful her presence always made him feel. Stretching out and resting his elbows on the work table next to the lamp he closed his eyes and said a silent prayer.

Jacob wanted things to work out with the shop for his mother's sake. He was unhappy about having to decide between work and Ruth; but realized that he could not commit to a relationship until things were more settled for himself and his family. It felt like he was being wrung from two ends; on one side were his responsibilities towards his family and on the other side was his affection for Ruth. It felt like he wasn't giving justice to either of them at the moment.

Lord, please help me out of this predicament.

He tried to focus on his prayers but he was too stressed out with the situation. He opened his eyes and looked at the workshop. He felt trapped under the obligation of his duties. It felt as if the walls were closing in on him.

Jacob banged his fist in frustration. The lamp at the edge of the table wobbled and as he watched in disbelief, it tottered off the edge and fell on the floor with a crash. The kerosene spilled over the floor covered with wood scraps and sawdust and immediately caught fire. There was no time to react and he watched as the debris ignited into a fast spreading flame.

No! Jacob stood up and raced to find a can of water. He couldn't find any. He ran out of the wood shop calling for Isaac and searching for water. Isaac was nowhere to be found and the smell of burning wood left a sickening feeling in the pit of his stomach.

Chapter 6

"Isaac!" Jacob hollered running frantically toward the house. "Fire! There's a fire... *Mudder!*"

He stopped just as he got to the side of the house, grabbed a bucket and filled it with water. Isaac was still nowhere to be found.

"Isaac!" he shouted again grabbing the bucket and racing back to the workshop. Smoke was bellowing out of the two small side windows that were the only ventilation in the wooden structure. Jacob peered through the door only to find that the fire was spreading quicker than he'd thought. He hurriedly tossed the water onto the flames then ran back to the house where he found Miriam and Isaac scrambling to the yard.

"Jacob, what's going on?" Isaac asked

looking at him, then up at the dark clouds of smoke rising from the work shop. "Good heavens!"

Miriam stood frozen on the spot.

"We need to try to save as much as we can," Jacob instructed Isaac. Isaac sprang into action and they both dipped their buckets into an overflowing water drum to fill them and ran back to the workshop.

"We need to hurry!" Jacob said feeling the enormous weight of the disaster that was now unfolding. Where were the neighbors? They were always outside and ready to help out at a moment's notice but today of all days there was not a single soul to be seen outside of their farm. The flames were getting bigger and bigger by the second.

"This isn't working, we need more man

power!" Jacob said throwing another bucket of water onto the flames. Isaac raced up behind him and did the same, then Miriam.

"*Mudder*, get the neighbors!" Jacob called.

"Good Lord, help us!" Miriam cried. "They went off to town this morning; I don't think anyone is at home!"

Suddenly Jacob spotted two men running onto their farm.

"Where's the fire?" one of them shouted from a distance.

"Over here in the workshop!" Miriam called, and then the men came racing to where they stood. All four ran back and forth filling buckets, and trying to douse the flames. Sweaty and covered in soot they stopped short at the sound of a window blowing out. The flames had spread out to the roof and deep down inside

Jacob realized the kerosene-drenched wood would burn relentlessly no matter what they did. The help was not enough.

The fire raged mercilessly and they all stood watching as the flames ripped through the workshop. Jacob felt like his entire life and the memories of his father were being gutted by the fire. He searched for Miriam and found her sobbing in Isaac's arms.

Jacob let out a tormented cry.

*****

Jacob lay on his bed staring at the ceiling. The workshop was gone. The fire had spread fast and had left nothing but destruction in its wake. Jacob and Isaac had only been able to save a few of the antiques but Jacob knew those wouldn't do much good. The workshop had been the family's primary source of income and now it would be impossible to pay their debts.

He knew the creditors would come calling and that they needed to figure something out, and fast.

"When's the next installment due?" he asked Isaac who was sitting on a chair in a far corner of the room staring out the window. Jacob had no doubt that he was looking at the gutted debris of their workshop.

"Next week," Isaac said solemnly. He too was still in disbelief.

Jacob shook his head. "This is all my fault. I was irresponsible. Now we won't have money to pay them."

"Accidents happen," Isaac said simply.

"Why does this always happen to our family?" Jacob asked angrily. "It's my fault. If I had just swept..."

"Jacob," Isaac said quietly. "*Gott* is still here. He has a plan, I promise you."

"What plan?" Jacob blurted. He'd asked the question more to himself, than to Isaac.

"I am not sure about God's designs and why the workshop was burnt; but I do know that God will show the path when the time comes. We've come a long way, do not lose hope now."

With that Isaac got up and walked to the door. "Miriam needs us," he said before stepping out of the room, and shutting the door.

Jacob sighed. He wished he had unshakable faith like Isaac. Now he could only question himself. Why had he been so distracted lately? He'd been so happy to see Ruth, and then so devastated that he in his uncertainty was causing her so much pain that he'd allowed his emotions to get the best of him. Again. Why was all of this happening? He'd barely recovered from the death of his father and now it felt like a series of unfortunate events was unfolding that he had no control over. Jacob felt anger and guilt creeping up inside. He didn't want to feel any of those emotions again. In the midst of his hopelessness Isaac's words for some reason stuck in his head.

God will show the path.

Isaac's words reminded him that unquestionable faith in the Lord would eventually be manifested in having a blessed life. He looked outside at the sky. Jacob knew he was being tested. He fell to his knees and prayed.

Chapter 7

Miriam sat in a rocking chair looking out the window onto the barn. The conversation happening all around her sounded distorted, and she could hardly believe what was happening.

"We will help you raise a new work shop," a gruff voice belonging to Luke, one of the two neighbors who'd helped them to extinguish the fire said.

"We will get the word to everyone and have the new workshop up and running in no time," the other neighbor Amos said nodding eagerly.

Jacob and Isaac were standing across the room from Miriam, and the wives of the two men were seated around a small table in the middle of the room. They were discussing rebuilding the family workshop in a traditional barn raising manner.

"Thank you for your gracious offer," she heard Isaac saying. "We really appreciate all your help."

"No need to thank us," Luke said. "Eli would've done the same for us."

The name of her late husband snapped Miriam back to reality. The workshop had gone up in flames and there was nothing anyone could do to change what had happened. What she needed to do now was thank God that no one had been hurt. She was sitting in a room filled with people who cared about her and her family's future, and she was grateful.

*****

"Will you take care of the workshop again Jacob?" his mother asked.

Jacob stood in a corner of the room rocking back and forth on the heels of his shoes. Did his family really expect him take up his father's responsibility again? He'd almost burnt down their entire house and feared another mishap. He stood there silently, then finally spoke up.

"*Mudder*, I am not sure I'll be able to manage the workshop."

His mother looked surprised.

"Why not?" she asked.

Jacob shrugged and looked down at the floor boards.

"I thought you liked carpentry work," his mother tried again.

Jacob shook his head. "I don't want another mishap."

"Jacob, what happened yesterday could have happened to anyone," his mother said.

"It's even happened to me one time," Luke piped up. "By some stroke of luck the flames didn't spread as quickly as this one, but you never know."

Jacob didn't know what to say. He could still picture the flames eating away at everything his father had left behind. It was as though his father himself had been saying a final good bye. He cleared his throat and looked away.

"I want to help but... I don't know *Mudder*. It's not a good idea."

"Alright," his mother said looking disappointed.

"I'll do it," Isaac said.

Both Miriam and Jacob looked at him in

surprise. Jacob wondered why he was volunteering. Then he realized that with his refusal, Isaac remained the only other alternative. *Am I shying away from my responsibilities?* He didn't have an answer to it.

"That would be a big help," their mother said. "Are you sure?"

Isaac nodded.

Miriam looked relieved, and Luke patted Isaac on the shoulder.

"We'll get started this week," Luke said.

*****

"The neighbors have agreed to help us," Jacob informed Uncle Miller. He'd driven two hours back to his uncle's farm to deliver the bad news.

Uncle Miller and Aunt Martha were

saddened to hear about the fire. Just like Isaac, they reiterated that accidents happened and Jacob shouldn't take the event too close to his heart. His uncle was sure that things would sort out in the end.

"We'll help out where we can too," Uncle Miller said. "I'll come by the farm in the morning with supplies."

"Thank you uncle," Jacob said.

"Don't worry son," Uncle Miller said. "Worry never did anybody any good."

Jacob sighed and his aunt reached out and ruffled his hair in the same way she'd always done when he was a child.

"Thanks for coming by to let us know," Aunt Martha said. "Everything will be alright. Trust *Gott*."

*****

Ruth spotted someone who looked like Jacob coming up the road. She was just returning home from her friend Sarah's house where she'd gone to pick up some fruit, and couldn't believe her eyes. *Maybe I just miss him too much*, she thought, trying to shake the thought out of her head but as the stranger approached, she knew she couldn't be wrong.

"Jacob?" Ruth said looking at him in surprise. "What are you doing here?"

He walked straight up at her and appeared even more taken aback than she was.

"Ruth?" Jacob said. "I was just thinking about you."

"I didn't know you were back," she said putting one hand on her hip. Ruth always did that when she was irritated. She put her arm down and straightened her posture when it occurred to her how peculiar she might look.

"I'm not," he said.

"What do you mean?" she asked.

"I only came to see my uncle."

"Why didn't you come calling for me?" Ruth asked looking hurt.

Jacob sighed. "There's too much to tell you."

"What has happened?"

"There was a fire."

"A fire?" Ruth asked, wondering how she hadn't heard about it. "At your uncle's farm?"

"No, at my home."

"Oh no!" Ruth said. "I'm so sorry! When did this happen?"

"A couple of days ago. The workshop is gone."

Ruth closed her eyes and hugged him, then pulled away when she realized what she had done.

"I'm so sorry!" she said peeking out from one eye, and then the other. "I'm so sorry Jacob..."

"Don't be. I'll fix it. I'll fix the farm."

"Where are you going?

"Back to Uncle Miller's farm and then home."

"When will we meet then?"

"I don't know Ruth."

"How long is this going to go on for?" she asked. "You not knowing anything?"

She knew this wasn't the time or place to be scolding Jacob but she felt anger burning deep down inside. So much was going on with Jacob and he hadn't even bothered to tell her, let alone come see her.

"Ruth," Jacob said meeting her gaze. "I care for you. I want you to know that. I'm having a hard time right now. I think it would be best for me to focus on my livelihood, rather than on you and me."

*****

He looked away. Jacob knew his words would hurt her but didn't see any other way for things to move forward. The last thing he wanted to do was hurt Ruth, but he didn't want her to feel like he could be there for her. He watched as tears streamed down her face, tortured that he wouldn't be able to say anything that would comfort her.

"At least you should have cared enough to let me know how you were," she said quietly, then sobbed. He reached for her but she pulled away. Ruth looked at him one last time and stormed away.

Chapter 8

Maybe she had been hasty. The look in Jacob's eyes just before she'd stormed off had broken her heart. What was she to do? Stand there looking silly with tears running down her face?

She loved him. There wasn't a doubt in her mind about that and she regretted the way she'd handled things. Ruth could tell how hurt Jacob was about everything that was happening and she knew she hadn't made things any easier by accusing him of not caring about her.

Ruth walked around in circles in the middle of the road near her home. She was fighting the temptation to run back over to find Jacob and apologize. Maybe she'd go to the Millers' house. Making up her mind to make things right, Ruth headed to Uncle Miller's farm. She walked quickly and purposefully hoping to find Jacob before he went into the house, but caught a glimpse of him just as he walked into the barn. She walked past the gate to follow him, and stopped short just outside of the door. She could hear voices inside. It sounded like Jacob was inside the barn talking to someone.

Not knowing whether she should run away, or wait for him, Ruth stood bolted to the spot.

"I don't know what to do," she heard Jacob voice.

"This is a test of patience Jacob," another voice said. It was Uncle Miller's. "Don't give up just yet."

"I know uncle... but it's tough," he said.

"It's all part of growing up," Uncle Miller

said. "Sometimes when it feels like things are falling apart, it really is the way that everything comes together."

"I'm just worried about *mudder*," Jacob said. "She's gone through so much. We all have. I tried to keep things going with the workshop and I made a mess of things."

"We can't go through life thinking we can control everything Jacob," Uncle Miller said. "That's where we go wrong. When it starts feeling like things are out of control, sometimes that's when we have to let go and give it to God."

There was silence for a moment and Ruth feared that they'd come walking out of the barn. She moved into a corner where they couldn't see her, but their conversation continued.

"Uncle... I've hurt Ruth," Jacob said. "I

can't be there for her the way I would like to be. I'm no good at making a living for myself. I couldn't even keep things going in the workshop. My father was the best at carpentry, and I..."

"Jacob," his uncle said. "Pay less attention to the way things look on the surface, and more to the promises of God. These challenges are meant to build you up. If Ruth is the one for you then it will happen. Give it time."

Jacob said nothing, and Uncle Miller kept talking. "You learn by doing Jacob. It is not going to happen overnight."

"Thank you uncle."

"We will pray together before you head off."

"Yes uncle."

Ruth heard shuffling feet and pressed her back against the wall. By some stroke of luck Uncle Miller walked out of the barn and headed in the other direction. He was holding a bag of chicken feed, and Ruth knew he was headed for the fields.

She breathed a huge sigh of relief, and in the next instant she was standing face to face with Jacob. Inhaling sharply she took a few steps back and tried to compose herself.

"I'm sorry, I didn't mean to listen," Ruth said quickly. "I saw you go in and... and I didn't want to leave and then not see you and..."

Jacob put a finger to his lips. "It's alright."

"Jacob... I'm so sorry," she said feeling fresh tears welling up at her eyes.

"It's okay Ruth," he said looking

concerned. "Please don't cry."

"What can I do to help you?" she asked, her voice breaking.

"Ruth..." he said putting his hand on her shoulder and looking her in the eye. "I want to be there for you. I want to take care of you, but I can't. Not right now. Maybe I am not the right person for you."

Ruth looked at Jacob standing there looking defeated and felt a surge of emotion. She felt guilty at being angry with him, when she could obviously see him struggling against the unfortunate string of events that were plaguing him ever since his father died. Ruth was glad she had returned to see how he was doing. He needed all the support at the moment and she would do her utmost to help him tide through the crisis.

"It will take some time to adjust to the role of breadwinner," she told him. "I understand..."

"No," Jacob said abruptly. "You are everything a woman should be. You will be well cared for. I just don't know what to do."

Jacob took a step back. "Come inside and see Aunt Martha," he said gesturing to the house. He started walking and Ruth followed him thinking the whole way of how much she loved him. She loved him but she couldn't convince him that love was enough. A man was meant to provide for his family and until Jacob was convinced that he was capable of doing that they would have no future.

Chapter 9

Ruth didn't spend a long time at the Miller's house. She knew her parents would have been wondering where she was so she'd politely greeted Jacob's aunt, stuck around for a slice of pie, and left long before Uncle Miller returned promising to visit again soon. Ruth liked Aunt Martha. The woman treated her like her own daughter and Ruth could tell that the older woman thought she'd make a good wife for Jacob. While Ruth knew the final decision and the blessing they needed to move forward had to come from both their parents, she hoped Aunt Martha would at least be able to talk some sense into Jacob.

Ruth walked into her house and almost crashed into her brother Abram who was running around the house chasing Mary.

"Leave me alone Abram or I'm going to tell *Mudder*!" Mary said looking annoyed.

She stomped off toward her room and Abram followed.

"You can't make me," he said sticking out his tongue and smiling. Ruth laughed at her sister's plight.

"If you don't stop following me I'm going to lock you out of our room," Mary warned giving Ruth the eye for not intervening.

"Abram," Ruth said still laughing. "Please, leave Mary alone. She's had enough of you. Why don't you go play outside in the garden?"

Abram sighed and threw his hands in the air. "Sisters are no fun.

Ruth and Mary both laughed as he

walked out to the garden with a sulk.

"Thank you *schweschder*," Mary said looking relieved. "*Mudder* and father are looking for you. They're out in the barn."

Ruth walked away from her sister and headed outside after Abram. She passed him examining the flowers and waved as she walked by. Her mother and father were sitting on a bench outside the barn. She greeted them and sat down.

"Ruth, we were just asking Mary for you," her mother said. "Did you know that Jacob is in town? I thought I spotted him on the way back from the market."

"Yes *mudder*. He is back."

Her parents both looked surprised and she knew they would ask why he hadn't come calling for her.

"There was a fire," Ruth said quickly. "At the farm where he lives with his mother. They lost the workshop. It was a disaster. Jacob is upset about that."

"*Ach* no!" her father said shaking his head. "I knew something had to be the matter when he didn't come by the farm."

"I'm so sorry to hear this Ruth," her mother said. "We should really go over to see his family."

Ruth nodded in agreement, and made plans with her parents to go see Jacob's family before nightfall.

*****

"I don't know if this is a good idea," Jacob said looking at the floor. Ruth and her family had come over to show their support in light of the fire, and now their relationship was up for discussion.

"Son, it is clear that you like our daughter," Ruth's father said. "We think you are a fine young man, and would make a good husband for her. Why are you changing your mind now?"

Jacob was having a hard time finding the right words. Ruth's mother and father both looked disappointed. Uncle Miller and Aunt Martha looked at him expectantly, waiting to hear what he had to say.

"I care for Ruth, but I don't know what my destiny is," Jacob said finally. "Or if Ruth and I can have a future together."

"What do you mean?" her father asked.

"I am not yet able to care for Ruth the way a husband should," Jacob said. "I do not wish my situation upon her."

"Jacob, I understand you," Ruth's father said with a small smile. "What you must remember though is that your destiny is with *Gott*. Pray for enlightenment and you will find the answers you need."

Ruth's mother nodded. "Pray to *Gott* and he will set your path straight."

Jacob realized they were right. It was what everyone from Isaac to his uncle had reiterated. He had to surrender himself to God. He remembered when he had first arrived at his uncle's place, how shaken his faith in God had been. And then he had help from Ruth in restoring his belief. He had promised himself at that time that he would not let go the path of faith.

It was true he had prayed to God, but he was still trying to control his fate. But what did he know of God's plan for him?

Trust in the Lord with all your heart and lean not on your own understanding; in all your ways submit to Him, and He will make your paths straight. Jacob remembered the lines from the Bible.

God will show the path, he told himself.

*****

Jacob spent the entire night praying. He'd woken up in a peaceful state of mind. He had finally realized that it was not up to him to decide his destiny when a power greater than him was sculpting his future. He looked out of the window. It was early dawn and the sun hadn't come out yet.

Jacob got out of bed, washed his face and headed over to Ruth's family's farm where he found her in the stable tending to the horses. He hadn't been to the farm in a while and she looked surprised to see him.

"What are you doing here?" she asked.

"I came to apologize. I'm really sorry Ruth."

"What for?"

"I'm sorry for being so distant."

"I understand Jacob. No need to apologize."

Jacob stood quietly and watched as Ruth brushed one of the horses.

"No, I want you to hear this. I've doubted God for far too long. It has only resulted in disaster. I do not want to lose you. I have every confidence that God will show us how to make this right."

Ruth smiled. "I have prayed also Jacob."

She looked up at the horse she was

grooming, then back at Jacob.

"Come and help me," she said simply, and he walked over and helped her wash the horses and clean out the stables. When they were done they sat on a bench barely big enough for two people and talked until the sun came up.

"It's a beautiful morning. Will you come on a buggy ride with me?" Jacob looked at Ruth.

Ruth blushed as if she could read his thoughts. She nodded. Jacob felt grateful that Ruth had stuck with him through thick and thin. *Trust is the other name of love,* he realized as he looked at her beautiful face. He was happy to be in her company.

They walked over to the Millers and got into the buggy. The horse sauntered at a gentle pace. Jacob didn't have any particular destination in mind. He looked over at her occasionally, but she was quiet enjoying the serenity of the early morning. He stopped in the middle of a lush field admiring the greenery of the grass that contrasted with the azure blue of a cloudless sky.

Jacob turned towards her. The morning light was shining across her face, and he never felt so truly happy. He smiled involuntarily.

"What?" Ruth's voice broke his thoughts. Jacob realized that he had been staring unabashedly at her.

"I am sorry. It's just…" he didn't know what to say.

"Just what?" Ruth asked and Jacob detected a slight tease in her voice. She was just making fun of him. She knew why he had asked her out in the buggy. He reached out and held her hand. He was rewarded by seeing a fresh smile bloom on her face.

"There comes a time in a young man's life when he desires to be united in marriage to a fine woman." Jacob looked at her. "You are a fine young woman, Ruth." He paused and then continued.

"Will you do the honor of being my wife?"

Chapter 10

"I think our children will be a good match for each other," Ruth's mother Emma Byler said, and Miriam nodded. Jacob's parents had come a long way to see her, and she was grateful. She too felt it was time Ruth and Jacob settled down and was happy that his parents agreed.

"I think so too," Miriam said. Jacob had informed her mother about Ruth when he had returned. He had told her about how he'd met Ruth and she had helped him with his faith. Miriam had been pleased that Ruth had been able to talk some sense into Jacob. Miriam knew that Jacob needed a strong woman of faith to guide him, and was happy that he had found Ruth.

Ruth and Jacob watched as their parents talked about them as though they were not in the room.

"We just have to fix some things first," Miriam said. "Do you know about the fire?"

"We do," Mrs. Byler said. "We were sorry to hear about that. How is everything going?"

"We're making slow progress," Miriam said. "But I am worried about the creditors. They will come tomorrow."

"*Ach*," said Ruth's father. "Can you not explain to them about the fire? I am sure if you told them about the loss caused by the fire, they will understand."

"I hadn't thought of that," Miriam stopped. It had never occurred to her to go to the creditors and explain the situation. They should surely understand and empathize with the situation. She looked up at Isaac. "Isaac, can you go into town to speak with them?"

"Sure. I will." Isaac got up and was out of the house in a minute.

"They will be married in December," Miriam looked at the Bylers. "You have my blessings."

*****

A knock at the door in the afternoon scared Jacob out of his skin. He expected to find Isaac at the door returning from his trip to town but instead he found Mr. Wofford.

"Jacob!" the cheery old man said. "How are you son?"

Jacob smiled. He was happy to see a familiar face.

"I am well sir. How are you?"

"Hanging in there! I got some good news and I wanted to share it with you right away, but I went to the workshop to pick up some antiques and..."

Jacob sighed.

"I had no idea," Mr. Wofford said. "I am so sorry."

"It's alright. It will be up and running soon enough."

Mr. Wofford smiled again. "Well that at least is good news."

"I've got something for you though," Jacob said. "Give me a moment."

Jacob walked back into the house and found the few antiques he'd managed to salvage from the fire.

"I kept these for you," he said to Mr. Wofford lugging the antiques to the front door. "I was able to save these from your last order, but I'm afraid I'm not going to be able to make the next lot."

"Wonderful!" Mr. Wofford said with a wide smile. He and Jacob carried the antiques out to his buggy and when they were done the older man looked at him with excitement in his eyes.

"Now for my good news," he said. "My partners are looking for a horse breeder for their Midwest ranches. When I heard them I immediately thought about you. Would you by any chance be interested in supplying them with the horses?"

Jacob's eyes lit up.

"*Ach Wunderbaar!*" he said. "Of course."

He always forgot himself when speaking to *Englischers* and he felt slightly embarrassed when Mr. Wofford started laughing.

"That's great Jacob," The older man said. "I couldn't imagine someone better suited for the job than you. When they told me they needed someone I recommended you right away."

"Thank you Mr. Wofford."

"No, thank you!" Mr. Wofford said gesturing to his newly acquired antiques. "I'm sorry to hear about the shop. Such a legacy in your father's name that was."

"He'll live on in our memories," Jacob said.

"That he will," Mr. Wofford said. "This breeding work is right up your alley. I will let them know you're interested Jacob."

"Thanks Mr. Wofford," Jacob said waving him off once again. He was overjoyed for a new opportunity to do something he loved.

Just as soon as Mr. Wofford pulled off, Jacob spotted Isaac running toward him.

"Jacob... Jacob!" his brother called. "The creditors have agreed! They've agreed to be flexible with the payments in light of what has happened!"

Jacob hugged his brother and they jumped up and down like children. When they settled down Jacob looked up to the sky and thanked God.

Epilogue

Ruth was going to be his wife. The thought alone took his breath away. He watched her from a distance as she floated around the room in her new blue linen dress looking more beautiful than he'd ever seen her. Jacob couldn't stop smiling. After today he'd no longer be a single man, but a husband. Then they'd start a family of their own. Time had gone by so quickly but Jacob couldn't have been happier. For the first time in a long time it felt like everything was coming together.

"How are you feeling Jacob?" Uncle Miller said as he walked past on his way to find Aunt Martha.

"*Wunderbaar* uncle," Jacob smiled.

"See how things come together?" his uncle said merrily. "Sometimes you just have to wait, and trust God."

"You're right about that. Thank you uncle. To God be the glory."

"I'm proud of you," Uncle Miller said with a smile.

Jacob's heart was full as he watched his uncle walk away. He wished his father had been there to witness this day, and he searched for Miriam and found her looking at him, swiping away happy tears. Jacob walked toward her and gave her a hug. For once, Miriam was speechless. She looked up at him teary eyed as though she were about to say something but changed her mind and smiled.

"I know *mudder*," Jacob said. "He would have loved to be here today."

He parted ways with his mother, and searched for Ruth. The last few months had been challenging but today he was filled with hope. He was more grateful than he'd ever been for all his struggles as without them, he knew he'd never have managed to mature into the man he was today. With Ruth at his side they'd already made it through some of the tougher moments, and now they were here together. He spotted her and their eyes locked. She wore no makeup, but he had never seen another woman as beautiful as she.

*****

Ruth's eyes found Jacob's and she felt her heart drop. She was so excited that she didn't know what to do with herself. They'd waited until after the harvest for their wedding and now it was the first Tuesday in December. It was snowing outside in the fields, but she felt a warm glow within her. Trying to contain her excitement she looked from Jacob to the crowd as he approached, happy to find that all the people she cared about were there. She'd waited for this day her entire life, and now she was about to marry the love of her life.

The thought made her nervous. Ruth fiddled with her dress, then stuck her arms firmly to her sides. She looked up and found Jacob standing in front of her and his smile gave her all the reassurance she needed. The Bishop appeared, and Ruth and Jacob exchanged their vows before the community. When they were pronounced man and wife, Jacob touched her face and pulled her close. Holding her at arm's length and looking at her as though he still couldn't believe she was his wife, Jacob wrapped his arms around her and kissed her softly. In that moment, no one existed beyond their union, and Ruth thanked the heavens for the blessing of a new beginning.

THE END

38528107R00156

Made in the USA
Lexington, KY
08 May 2019